BUCHANAN'S
STOLEN
RAILWAY

Fawcett Gold Medal Books
by Jonas Ward:

BUCHANAN CALLS THE SHOTS

BUCHANAN GETS MAD

BUCHANAN ON THE PROD

BUCHANAN ON THE RUN

BUCHANAN SAYS NO

BUCHANAN TAKES OVER

BUCHANAN'S BIG SHOWDOWN

BUCHANAN'S GAMBLE

BUCHANAN'S GUN

BUCHANAN'S REVENGE

BUCHANAN'S SIEGE

BUCHANAN'S STOLEN RAILWAY

BUCHANAN'S TEXAS TREASURE

GET BUCHANAN

THE NAME'S BUCHANAN

ONE MAN MASSACRE

TRAP FOR BUCHANAN

BUCHANAN'S
STOLEN
RAILWAY

Jonas Ward

A FAWCETT GOLD MEDAL BOOK • NEW YORK

BUCHANAN'S STOLEN RAILWAY

© 1978 CBS Publications, The Consumer Publishing Division of CBS, Inc.
All rights reserved

ISBN 0-449-13977-8

Printed in the United States of America

10   9   8   7   6   5   4   3   2   1

BUCHANAN'S STOLEN RAILWAY

1.

BUCHANAN rode the big black horse up the Black Range marveling at the shining rails. Only three feet between them, they curved gracefully around the winding trail which he had traveled often before. When the twist or turn had been too sharp, someone had cut into the mountainside in order to accomplish his purpose.

Buchanan, all six feet four and two hundred and fifty pounds of him, was impressed. He was not totally pleased. He decried the destruction of the privacy of an old hunting and fishing ground. Yet he knew the need for silver; it was boom time in that market. Far above, nine thousand feet high, a friend was waiting, and Buchanan was always one for aiding his friends.

Down a dizzying distance below he could see the peaks of oaks, cottonwoods, and tangled brush of the valley of the river. This was Victorio country and there had been blood spilled from here to the Mogollons for a hundred years as the Apaches fought each other and then the invading White Eyes. This was New Mexico, Buchanan's adopted home base.

It was growing cooler at this altitude. He tipped his hat to one side of his sandy-red head and rode to a sharp turn, where he dismounted to dig out a jacket to cover his woolen shirt and loose checkered vest. He wore his six-gun in the mountains, respecting snakes and small animals that, wild and unafraid, might snap at the heels of Nightshade, the black horse.

A sound around the bend of a mighty cliff which had been blasted for the progress of the rails distracted him. He moved upward, silent in his worn El Paso hand-stitched boots. Keeping close to the scarred rock, he removed his hat and peered cautiously around the sharp corner.

There were a dozen Apaches busy at attacking the rails. Using primitive tools and limbs cut from oaks, they were having little luck—but in time they would succeed, he knew. He looked them over with care before he stepped into view. He did not draw his six-gun.

He said, "Now, Vicenzio, what's this? Don't

you know the war is over, the peace treaty signed?"

The young man addressed came up with a round rock and threw it with amazing speed and skill. Buchanan thrust up his left hand and caught it just before it struck his skull.

"That's what I get for teachin' you to throw a baseball," he said reprovingly. "Now you-all stand up in a line and let me look you over."

Vicenzio was just out of his teens, a full warrior. He was slim, built from an old mold—not squat like most of the others—with flashing eyes, an aquiline nose, long, strong legs. He was a throwback to Mangus Colorado, from whom he was descended.

He said, "Buchanan, it is you."

"You might've looked before you chucked that rock," Buchanan said. "Could've doggone near killed a fella."

Vicenzio said to his companions, "Do as he says; he is a friend."

They lined up. They were mainly short, strongly built Apaches. There were two or three girls in the crowd; all were youthful. Their black eyes remained full upon Buchanan.

Vicenzio went on, "The iron horse will scare away the game. It has been a bad time in the hills, Buchanan. They took our copper; now they take our silver. The old men are afraid; they are finished. Something must be done."

"Yeah, maybe. I know you're right." Buchanan sighed. "But it's the way of the world. Thought they taught you that in school, Vicenzio."

"They talked. I listened."

"And you learned there was no use fightin' any more. Suppose you tear up a few rails. You think Longbo won't put 'em back again?"

"Longbo Stone has troubles," Vicenzio said. "The more trouble we can give him, the better we protect the Black Hills, our country."

"Part of it's your country. This here trail, your people built it, used it. But Victorio signed it away. I ain't sayin' it was right. Seems like politicians never keep their promises—never did, never will. But it's the way things are." Buchanan spoke in discouraged tones. "If it would help any, I'd turn to and work with you. But you're better off with a man like Longbo up yonder at his mine. He ain't bad folks."

Vicenzio nodded once. "He is better than most. But his business, that is bad."

"He built a smelter down below. He's got to get his ore down there to the mill. So he put in the rails," Buchanan said. "He asked the Apaches for help."

They all groaned at the very thought of Apaches working at menial labor. Buchanan held up his hand.

"I know. But anyway, he did ask. Then he

brought in the Chinese. And he had to feed them and the Irish gandy dancers and all. It ain't been easy for Longbo."

"He is alive," flashed Vicenzio. "Many a night I lay watching and could have killed him."

"And started another war."

Vicenzio made a despairing gesture. "So I did not kill him."

"Do your people need food right now?" Buchanan asked.

"We have meat. We have no money for other needs."

Buchanan took a gold piece from his pocket. "Now, you go and get what you need, and we'll see about what happens tomorrow or next day. Like I always told you at the mission school: Day by day, that does it."

Vicenzio hesitated. There were growls from among his followers. He said, "You promise, Buchanan?"

"I promise to do all I can for your bunch."

The handsome youth turned to the others. He accepted the gold coin, held it high. "Buchanan is my friend. He was always the friend of the Apache. We will go now and wait."

It seemed to Buchanan that they were not too unhappy to cease their labors. They tossed their makeshift tools into the canyon. Vicenzio watched them go, vanishing like lizards into the mountain. Then he came toward Buchanan.

"I am glad I did not hit you with the rock."

"You were some kind of ball playin' kid," Buchanan said. "Best I ever saw."

"Those days are past."

"Men are making money playing baseball now," Buchanan told him. "They have teams, banded together. They play for championships."

"It is of no interest. I am the leader now. The chiefs no longer lead. You will come to us?"

"If I can find you."

Vicenzio pointed upward to the west. "The old place. The high valley. You know it."

"I'll be there. And Vicenzio . . ."

"Yes?"

"You may be the leader and all. But you should've had a lookout around that bend where I came in."

Vicenzio bowed his head. "I was in the school too long. You shame me, Buchanan."

Buchanan laghed. "Forget it. Get some supplies from town and I'll be seein' you later on."

The youthful Indian went as did the others, up the side of the mountain. Buchanan watched him, worrying, feeling guilt which he knew was not his alone.

He turned his mind to the days when Vicenzio had chosen to attend the mission school at Silver City. Baseball had been growing as a sport since the soldiers in the camps in the War between the States had converted it from the children's game "one old cat." Buchanan had played in his youth in East Texas, and now every town in the Far West had its team. Back in the East the leagues had formed and men actually used leather gloves on their hands to protect against the hard ball. Vicenzio had been the best kid Buchanan ever coached.

He whistled and Nightshade came around the corner of the cut, making his way carefully, distrusting the slippery steel rails, keeping close to the cliff side of the trail. "Trail?" thought Buchanan. "Now it's a railway. A little bitty one, but rails nevertheless."

He had harbored high hopes for Vicenzio, he reflected. He thought the boy would grow to be a teacher, that the gap between the Apache— the People—and the white man would be somehow altered by the efforts of such young men. He had been wrong, he now realized. The chasm was too wide. The pride of the red man was too deep. The stupidity and callousness of the white invader was too great.

Nightshade wandered slowly upward and onward. The road would straighten, then go into a convolution of swerves and twists. That Longbo Stone had been able to build the railway was a matter of wonderment.

At last they came to the high valley. All the huge mountains in the area could boast of such quiet, peaceful places where deer came to eat out of proffered hands—white tail, fantail, and mule deer—where bobcats and mountain lions and coyotes once roamed freely, fighting the war for survival among themselves. Now they were gone, driven away by man. Ahead he could see the entrance to the Longbo Mine, a big hole in the side of a mountain. Little gondola cars stood in a row on a sidetrack, a caboose attached at the end. Two or three men worked at various small chores. They paid Buchanan no attention.

At the head of the rails that led down the Black Range stood a little steam engine, all bright and shiny, wearing the number 69 on its prow. It weighed, Buchanan knew, only a little over six tons. Still, it was sturdy and strong—he had checked it all out before coming on this journey. He knew the cost—$8500.

He knew Longbo Stone did not have that much money and could not raise it. Further, Longbo was already in debt.

Apart from the mine and the rails, nestled close to the north side of the mountain was a cabin fashioned of lumber hewn from the high valley. It was one-storied but it was wide and deep. A stream coming down from above ran alongside it. It was the most elaborate mountain cabin that Buchanan had ever seen.

There was a stable, little more than a lean-to, Buchanan saw with disapproval. In a small corral a half dozen ordinary hacks nibbled at the furze in discontent. Longbo had never been a horseman.

Buchanan dismounted, trailing the reins, uncertain. He approached the cabin. A woman's voice, high and strong, beat upon his ears.

"I'm sick of it, you hear me? You've spent it all. You put all your eggs in one damn basket. I don't believe in any Buchanan. Where the hell is he?"

Buchanan cleared his throat, then called loudly, "Hallooo the house."

For a moment there was a profound silence, broken only by the chatter of a brave squirrel in a ponderosa. Buchanan went to the door of the house, which swung open. Framed in it was a man so tall and reedy thin that he looked like a clothespin. He had to incline his head to squint at Buchanan's six feet four.

"Tom! You got here."

"Said I would, didn't I? How goes it, Longbo?" He was trying to pretend he had not heard the voice of the woman.

"Fine, just fine. Now that you're here." There was anxiety in his voice despite his protests. "Come in, come on in."

The front room was huge. It was cluttered with furniture. The woman stood in its center. She was fully composed, a fixed smile on her lips. She was medium in height and shapely, what Buchanan's father would have called "a

15

fine figger of a woman." Her waist was slim, her bosom ample, her feet and hands small and shapely. Her eyes were dark and shrewd.

"You never met Dolly," Longbo was saying. He was somewhere between pride and frustration. "We only got married a year ago in Frisco."

"I heard. Congratulations," said Buchanan, bowing his head to the woman.

The lady had small, white, regular teeth when she smiled. She extended her hand, limp at the wrist. "Tom Buchanan, welcome to our home in the mountains."

Buchanan touched the hand, which was cold. "It's some palatial house for away up here!"

"I designed it. Bo built it. . . . I call him 'Bo.' Can't seem to say 'Longbo.' "

"Just a sort of joke name," Buchanan told her. "Just so you don't call him late for whiskey time."

She laughed, sharply, then sobered. "We don't have the help we need. Irish girl in the kitchen, a few Mex greasers around. My daughter, she's outdoors running wild I expect. It's all new to her. She's my child by a previous marriage, of course."

It seemed that she was trying to make a good impression and that it was a task. Buchanan sat in a chair she indicated, soft and wide and comfortable. The furnishings were more than good, they were lush.

Longbo said, "Here's plenty of good Monongahela for you, Tom. I remember it's your brand. Adah—that's Dolly's daughter—will be along."

Dolly Stone was a lady he thought he could understand. Her labored speech indicated she was city bred, probably in a school of hard knocks. He knew San Francisco and its demiworld. Many rich men had married ladies with a past. Longbo had joined the crowd.

Longbo produced a decanter and a bowl of ice. "Got an ice plant up here," he said proudly. "On account of it's so lonely for the gals we try to do things up brown."

Buchanan glanced at the finished walls, the draperies, the upholstered red plush furniture. Beyond was a dining room with a buffet loaded with silver, a long mahogany table, eight high-backed chairs. A wide swinging door led into a kitchen. "Looks mighty like a palace in the mountains."

"If we can't live in the city," said Dolly Stone, "we can at least enjoy what we have got."

"Uh-huh." There was no doubt where much of Longbo's capital had gone, he thought. The lady was wearing a few thousand dollars' worth of diamonds and pearls.

"That's what Dolly always says." Longbo beamed and poured whiskey. The lady took four ounces along with the men. "She's got great taste in things, Dolly has."

"Thank you, Beauregard." She sipped the whiskey, dimpled at them. Then she abruptly stood, glass in hand. "I leave all the business to my husband. I don't want to interfere in any way, Mr. Buchanan, so I will leave you alone together."

She swayed out of the room. There were evidently bedrooms to either side of the railroad-like center of the huge cabin-mansion. When she had gone, Longbo drained his glass, poured another.

"Well, we sure had times together, Tom. Here's to 'em."

Buchanan drank sparingly of the booze. "Uh-huh. And now you got troubles."

"Nothin' a few dollars won't clear up." Longbo's enthusiasm was genuine. "You seen that little beauty of an engine out there. Once that's paid for and I can get the ore a-rollin' down the mountain we'll all be rich."

"Eighty-five hundred dollars, you said in the telegram."

"That's it. Got to have it, Tom. It's the breakin' point. You get a tenth interest in the net profits if you come up with it."

"Tell me about it."

Longbo tossed off the drink. In the past he had been moderate with liquor, Buchanan remembered. Now he seemed feverish. When he spoke, his voice was sharp and high and slightly nervous. He told how he had found the lode of silver, how he had used all his money to drill it and put in the mill and the rails. He told of the miners he had hired and who were now waiting down below in the towns for him to start drilling again.

And he admitted he had run out of money and that the bankers were unwilling to advance any further funds.

"But if it's a good proposition, how come?" Buchanan asked.

Longbo's face elongated. His voice dropped. "You know Colin Masters?"

"Certainly I know Masters. Everybody knows him."

"He wants the mine."

Buchanan said, "Colin Masters needs the Longbo like he needs a shot in the rear end. He's got railroads, gold mines, cattle ranches, two newspapers, and what-all. Why should he want Longbo?"

"He ain't got silver and silver's boomin'. Colin just can't even hear a whisper about somethin' that he doesn't want it."

"There's other silver mines," Buchanan observed.

"Well, him and me . . . we sorta had a fallin' out."

"Uh-huh." Colin Masters was a man who fell out with many people. "Over what kind of a deal?"

"Dolly."

"Your wife?"

"Well . . . and his baseball team. You know about his baseball team?"

"I know he supports one. Best in the West. Calls them the Westerners. Spends a lot of time with 'em."

"Yeah. Travels around in a special car challengin' everybody. Never lost a game. So . . . well, after Dolly left him and—"

"Dolly was his girl?"

"Ahem. In a manner of speakin'." Longbo poured another drink. "Anyways, she left him for me and we went on our honeymoon back to Chicago and saw two real professional teams, the Cincinnatis and the Chicagos. Fella named Cap Anson. You never seen such baseball!"

"Yes, I did," Buchanan told him. "I was back there, too, last year, with Coco."

"Coco? Oh, sure, Coco Bean, the prizefighter. . . . How is he nowadays?"

"I'm meeting him in Silver when I leave here," said Buchanan. "Go on with your story."

"So me and Dolly come back and I got into a poker game. Colin, he came into the game braggin' about his team just beat Dodge City or some club. And I had to get big mouth about how the professionals would whup his Westerners ninety to nothin'."

"That was not very smart, Longbo." Buchanan now felt the need for a second drink. He poured and went on, "Colin thinks more of his baseball team than he does of at least one of the banks he controls."

"Well, he cussed me out and quit the game—and him behind a couple thousand at that."

"So then the banks cut you off."

"Between Dolly and the baseball," said Longbo glumly. "Reckon Colin got a big mad on at me."

"And he wants the mine?"

"He told people he was gonna get it from me." The tall man stiffened. "This is it, Tom. This here is my life's work. This is everything."

"Uh-huh," said Buchanan. He drank. "And I promised you the money. And you're one of my oldest and best friends."

"That's the facts."

Buchanan sighed and produced a folded piece of stiff paper. "Here's a bank draft. It about cleans me. But a promise is a promise."

"You don't sound too high on it, Tom." Longbo was injured. "You know you can trust me."

"To the end of the world."

"Then?"

"I don't trust Colin Masters to the end of a

short rein on a buckin' bronc," Buchanan said. "Have you got any guards around? Anyone lookin' out for this place?"

"Just Adah and me. And a few Mexican boys."

"I'll have a look-see tomorrow," Buchanan said. Then he blinked and added, "Adah? She's a lookout?"

"Adah, she's Dolly's daughter." Longbo was slightly evasive. "She's a smart one."

From behind Buchanan a light voice said, "Why, thanks, Longbo. Mighty nice of you."

Buchanan arose from the chair. The girl was willowy, slim, of medium height. She wore her dark hair close to her shapely head. Her brown eyes were wide-spaced. She wore men's riding breeches on long legs encased in boots. Her shirt was cut to her body, short-sleeved, displaying muscular forearms tapering to long fingers.

She said, "I'm Adah Smith." She laughed. "Ma claims my father was named Smith. Never did see him. You must be Tom Buchanan."

Her handclasp was surprisingly strong, solid. Buchanan looked into her eyes and saw shadows. She had adopted a light manner, but there were emotions close to the surface which were far from cursory.

"Pleased to meet you, Miss Adah," he said.

"I've been attending your horse. A beautiful animal. Ma was so busy building the house she

22

forgot to put up a decent stable. But he'll be all right."

"I do thank you," said Buchanan. "Nightshade thanks you. He needs some oats."

"He's got them." She went to the whiskey bottle. She poured two ounces into a glass and swallowed the drink without blinking. She spoke to her stepfather. "There's people out there. I couldn't see them but I could almost smell them. I took the long ride, down the side trail and around and back up. I saw tracks. I can't read 'em, but I know them when I see 'em."

Longbo said, "There's some Apaches around."

The girl kept her great dark eyes on Buchanan. "The Apaches are hungry but peaceful. Do you know how many men are employed by Masters?"

"Why . . . a whole heap, here and there."

"Thousands. More than he can count. Coolies, vaqueros, trainmen, reporters, bankers. And gunmen."

"Here, now, Adah," said Longbo. "Colin never got into nothin' like that."

She did not laugh, although the corners of her wide mouth twitched. "You never heard of the Manguez County War?"

"That wasn't Masters."

"Nor the Hidalgo Corners Massacre?"

"Girl, what are you sayin'? That's slander!"

The girl now moved closed to Buchanan. "Ma

23

lived with Colin Masters. You ever hear of little pitchers with big ears?"

"I ain't listenin' to none of this," cried Longbo.

Adah Smith said, "Then you better go tell Ma that you got the money before she gnaws her fingernails clean off. And I better talk some to Mr. Buchanan, here."

"Colin Masters is a businessman," Longbo blustered. Then he stopped, shook his head. Lines etched his cadaverous countenance. He went to a sideboard, took out another bottle of whiskey, and went through the door by which Dolly had exited the room.

Adah asked, "Mr. Buchanan, are you hungry?"

"It's a habit I got real young," he replied.

She led the way to the kitchen. A girl with Ireland written all over her freckled, open face began a curtsy, recognized Adah, grinned, and said, "Ach, I feared it was your mither."

"This is Mr. Buchanan. He's hungry," said the girl.

"There's a-plenty. Me name's Mary, sir." She went to the stove and busied herself with pots and pans.

There was a long trestle table. Adah indicated a chair, and Buchanan sat next to her. The girl spoke in a lowered voice, leaning toward him.

She was tense, hurried as though in fear of being interrupted.

"My mother is a fool. She don't appreciate your friend Longbo. All she knows is to spend money. Longbo is so much in love with her that he can't say no."

Buchanan said, "I already gathered that." He waved a hand. "This house, her jewelry, everything."

"But she has goodness in her." Adah bit her lip, then plunged on. "We were supported by Colin Masters. You'd find that out anyway; might's well tell you. When I was sixteen he attacked me. Ma sent me away to school, sold everything—but hung around until Longbo appeared. Is that enough for you to know?"

"You're tellin' me Colin Masters has got two reasons for wantin' the mine?"

"He only needs one."

"You're tellin' me he's a dangerous crook—and him one of the most respected men in the West?"

"I am."

Buchanan grinned at her. "I knew that all along."

Her eyes grew wide. "And you loaned money to Longbo?"

"He's a friend," Buchanan explained. "We've been in tights together. He's always been right with me."

"Well." She paused. "You are some kind of a man—like he keeps telling us."

"But not too bright, huh?" Buchanan laughed. Mary was setting a huge plate of meat and vegetables before him. "This country was built by men like Colin Masters and by some others. Masters and the Comstock Lode people and them, they got rich. How they did it is their business—and that of the law, the government, whatsoever. Longbo wants to be one of them."

"He's not crooked enough."

"That may well be."

"There are men out there right now, Buchanan. I know it. They are planning something against us."

"Could be."

"Can you stay around? Until Longbo gets the money to the bank and starts operations?"

Buchanan shook his head. "I got to meet Coco in Silver City. I don't hire out as a guard."

"Even for your friend?"

"Coco Bean is the best friend I got in the world," Buchanan told her. "Haven't seen him in a long time. He went back East to fight the world champion, but they wouldn't make the match. He needs me around at a time like this."

She half-closed her eyes. "Is there any way I can get you to stay?"

"Nope. Excuse me, food shouldn't be left standin'." He began to eat. The girl was too intense, he thought, too highly strung. She should not be up there at the mine. She should be among her own kind, young people. She should not take responsibility for things beyond her ken.

She twisted her hands together. "At least you know what's going on. I'll leave you to eat your meal."

She left the room abruptly, as though highly disturbed. Buchanan ate the excellent food. The Irish girl surveyed him with round eyes.

She said, "Adah's good."

"I expect so."

"Her ma hasn't a smidgen of sense."

"But Longbo's a good boss."

"Sure and he's wonderful."

Buchanan said, "You got some more of that elk meat?"

The girl said no more. He arose replenished and thanked her. His good sense told him he had made a bad investment of money he might some day need. He went out of the back door. It was twilight. Nightshade was under the lean-to and seemed contented enough. Buchanan took his saddlebags and his blanket roll and put them on the back steps outside the kitchen. He picked up his rifle. The sun faded fast in the high place. He prowled, wondering about the girl, curious as to what signs of invaders she might have seen.

Since she was a city girl, it must have been something obvious.

There were tall trees in the valley and hardy brush that endured through the bitter winters, hiding beneath the snow until the spring thaws. Yet there was not much real cover. Tomorrow he could again take a closer look. Meantime, he searched for Adah.

It was a dangerous place for interlopers. There was only one exit in case of discovery—down the trail which was now also the railway. He came to the silent steam engine at the end of track, the symbol of success if the Longbo Mine was to survive. The last glimmer of light vanished and there was immediate darkness.

The girl screamed.

There was the beginning fizzle of snapping sparks along a line leading to the steam engine. Buchanan yelled, "Stay where you are!"

He ran forward. He planted a solid heel on the running fire.

He swung up the rifle and moved to the front of the engine. There was the sound of clattering hoofs going pell mell down the trail. He fired several shots with no hope of hitting a target. It would let them know that the people at the mine were on the job, he thought.

He leaned down and followed the dead fuse with his hand. It led beneath the engine. Very carefully he removed a package.

The girl was coming out of the shadows. She was trembling. "I saw them, but I was afraid to call out."

"Just as well, way things turned out."

"They tried to blow it up!"

He said, "Let's go to the house."

The cabin blazed with the light of lamps. Longbo was running toward them, rifle in hand. He stopped when he saw Buchanan in the reflected glow.

"Adah was right. They're tryin' to ruin me."

"Let's go inside," said Buchanan.

Mrs. Stone was in the kitchen, shivering as though with the ague. Mary stood in a corner, her eyes bright, twisting her apron in reddened hands. These were not intrepid pioneers, thought Buchanan. He went to the long table and put down the package. Everyone jumped.

"Awful small," he observed.

"Is it dynamite?" asked Longbo.

"Expect so." Buchanan's huge hands were deft opening the bundle. He extracted one small stick of dynamite and a lot of paper wadding. "Too small," he added.

"That wouldn't do damage that couldn't be fixed," Longbo said. "They're tryin' to scare us."

"They did a good job," Buchanan said, eyeing the women. "What they want is the engine, the rails, the mine. The whole shebang. They don't want to hurt you all."

"They want to use my engine," Longbo cried. "That Colin Masters wants to destroy me."

"And me!" shrieked Dolly Stone. "I want to get out of here!"

Longbo stared at her. He seemed to turn to jelly at the recognition of her fear. "I don't know—you could go down with Tom, if you feel that way."

"You know I can't ride a horse!"

Buchanan asked, "How did she get up here?"

"In the caboose," said Longbo. "I . . . I built the cabin like she said. Then she come up with Number 69."

"We can go down that way," said Dolly Stone. "You can drive that engine. We can sell the place."

Longbo stiffened. "Sell? Quit? Now, Dolly, you know this is my life. You been with me in this."

The emotion in his friend's voice stirred something deep inside Buchanan. He said, "No use to panic. Masters is smart. Hurting you people would affect his dealin's in all his other business. This bluff with the dynamite proves it. Let me go down and talk to him."

Longbo brightened. "People listen to Tom. It may work."

Dolly Stone put the back of her hand to her mouth. Her eyes were, oddly, upon Adah.

The girl said slowly, "Mr. Buchanan is right.

I won't leave here, Ma. If Mary wants to go down, she can go and I'll take care of you. We've got a few men to do the hard work."

"Where are the men?" asked Buchanan.

"Hidin'," said Longbo. "They ain't hired to fight. They're miners—and they haven't been paid lately."

Buchanan said, "I'll take that draft down and deposit it for you. Then we'll see what happens."

"You . . . you'll still loan us the money?" quavered Dolly Stone. "You . . . you won't desert us?"

"I made a promise," Buchanan told her. She was, he saw, regaining composure. She must have faced critical situations in her previous life. Maybe she could stand up to this one. "Bo needs you here. I say we all get some sleep and talk it over in the morning."

"That's right," Longbo said quickly. "Things always look better in the morning."

"Well. . . ." But Dolly allowed him to lead her from the kitchen. She took one last look at her daughter, heaved a sigh, and was gone.

Adah was looking at the dynamite. "A warning. That's what it is. Next time—it could be enough to destroy us."

"You said it yourself," Buchanan said. "He's got thousands of people workin' for him. If he wanted, he could wipe you all out any time. He'll try—but he'll do it his way. Smart."

"What can we do?"

"Every man's got his weakness. Thing is, we got to find his."

The wide, dark eyes surveyed Buchanan. Some of the tension went out of the girl. "You'll try. I know you will. If Ma doesn't . . ." She broke off. "All right then. You go down and do what you can. I know Longbo is a tough man. It's just—he's sort of come to the end of his rope."

"He's a good man," said Buchanan. "Go to bed. It's been a hard day for you."

She hesitated, then for the first time she smiled. Her face lit up; she seemed younger than twenty for an instant, a child, believing. She touched his hand and said, "Let me show you where you can sleep."

It was another big room, with an ample bed even for Buchanan. She left him, still smiling through her fears. He went for his bundle and closed the door and sat on a rawhide chair. Slowly he removed his clothing, poured water from a stone pitcher into a basin, and washed himself all over as best he could. No use to unpack, he would be leaving to meet Coco Bean at the railway station in the morning.

He blew out the lamp and got into the comfortable bed. He lay awake, thinking over the situation at the Longbo, thinking of Colin Masters.

He could picture the financier across a poker table some time back, a small man with a gambler's thin mustache. But he was not a big gambler nor a particularly good one at cards. His game was the big money, the trickeries of the business world. He had been born in the early days of Buena Vista, now San Francisco. His father had been a man of some wealth, and Colin had been a millionaire at twenty-one. He was now in his early thirties. He worked hard and he played hard and his big love, as Buchanan had said, was baseball.

He had gathered the "Westerners" from all over the country, paid them well. They traveled in a private train meeting all comers. As far as Buchanan knew they were undefeated this season.

It was a unique hobby in the West, although the game was spreading all over the country now. Most of the teams were pickup; Masters had no trouble with them. While his men were semiprofessionals, they were too good for the yet unorganized Western nines.

Buchanan had played the game since he was a button in East Texas. Now and then he had filled in on various town teams as catcher and power hitter. He was fond of baseball. He fell asleep thinking of fun in the past—plus worriment about Longbo and the mine, and the troubled young girl named Adah.

2.

THE copper was at Santa Rita, but Silver City was the biggest town in the area. Buchanan put up Nightshade at the Bull's Eye Livery Stable with Jess Chambers, an old friend. The train, he learned, was late.

Chambers said, "Colin Masters come in with his private car and fouled things up. Wish that son would stay on the Coast where he belongs.'"

"Masters is here?"

"Puttin' up his damn ball team at the hotel. They kowtow to that man and his bums wherever they go."

Buchanan said, "Now that's plumb interestin'. Now about the Santa Rita team? They goin' to play the Westerners?"

"Masters wants the game. I dunno. One thing he don't own is the diggin's at Santa Rita."

"If he's got his mind made up, he'll wangle a ball game somewheres. You got a team here, y'know."

"They stink," Chambers said. "Those hired players of his'n, they're hell on a town. Stick 'em in jail, he bails 'em out."

"Abe Catlow will throw 'em back in again," said Buchanan. "Abe don't back down for anybody."

"Abe's a good sheriff," admitted Chambers. "But I dunno. Masters is powerful set in his evil ways."

"He's got the banks and the railroads with him," admitted Buchanan. "Well, we will see what we will see."

"Nothin' good comes out of Masters. Try and tell people, they think you're crazy. But it's true."

"You and me, we know about him." Buchanan waved to the oldtimer and walked down the main street.

As he came abreast of the hotel, a tangle of men came hurtling out the saloon door, across the long verandah, and down onto the walk. He recognized Sheriff Abe Catlow. The others were flashily dressed individuals of various sizes, all loud and drunken.

Buchanan reached out and began sorting

them. He banged one head against another, deposited the victims in the gutter. A big man slashed at him, and Buchanan knocked him back up onto the porch. Catlow came up tangled with the last of them, a burly man with a scarred face. He broke loose. Buchanan cold-cocked the fellow. The sheriff was breathing hard and sporting bruises. He hit one of the men with his fist and slammed another so he ran into Buchanan, who neatly knocked him out with a right-hand punch.

Catlow peered, then said, "Thanks, Buchanan."

"Kinda early in the day for such shenanigans, Sheriff," said Buchanan.

"Not so early; they been at it all night."

Buchanan examined them more closely as they struggled to regain equilibrium. "Baseball fellas, huh?"

"Colin Masters," said Catlow, a man of few words.

Buchanan, as was his custom, was not wearing his gun in town. "Want some help?"

"Jail's right across the street."

Buchanan addressed the dazed ballplayers. "It'll be real nice if you walk peaceable over yonder and take a rest, maybe a little sleep."

The scar-faced man said, "The hell with you."

Buchanan sighed, took him by the collar of his fancy shirt and heaved him into the middle of the street. The others, shaking their heads, blinked, then meekly arose and lined up.

Catlow said, "Reckon you can just watch, now."

"Uh-huh," said Buchanan.

The Sheriff motioned, collared the scarred one en route, dragging him. They all marched into the hoosegow without further incident.

A calm voice behind him said, "I see you're still in trim, Buchanan."

Colin Masters was dressed in stovepipe striped trousers, patent leather boots, a long black coat, and a frilled shirt adorned with a single large pearl. A diamond glittered on the third finger of his left hand. He twirled a cheroot and smiled without mirth.

Buchanan said, "How do those boys of yours manage to play baseball? They go down like tenpins in a bowlin' alley."

"When drunk," replied Masters. "When they sober up, you might protect your back."

"Bad, are they?"

"Playful. But on to greater thoughts. I hear you've been up to visit your friend Stone."

"You hear just about everything, don't you?"

"If I'm interested." He inhaled smoke, blew it out through his nostrils. "You drew $8500 from your bank, for instance. Just the price of Engine 69."

"I'll have a word with my banker about that

piece of information leakin' out."

"Not his responsibility," said Masters airily. "Word gets around."

"In your circles, I reckon it does."

"You shouldn't get mixed up with Stone." The voice had suddenly changed. It contained ice in large buckets. The eyes, peculiar in their brightness, were slate gray, boring into Buchanan.

Along the rails a whistle blew a siren wail. Buchanan shrugged. "Uh-huh, reckon you'd say that. Right now I got to meet a friend. Talk to you sometime, Colin."

As he went toward the station the man called after him, "Nobody walks away when I've got something to say, Buchanan."

"I just did," said Buchanan over his shoulder. He did not look back.

The usual idlers were waiting in the station. Buchanan stood watching the train pull in. He had not seen Coco in months and he had honestly missed his friend. The brakes squealed, the chug-chug died with a sigh. The conductor swung down and doors of the coaches opened.

There was no way to miss Coco Bean, the black champion, a couple inches shorter than Buchanan and just as wide, long arms swinging, then reaching out to grab his partner.

"Tom! Hey there!"

"How's with you, Coco?" He looked over the

shoulder of the champion and added, "Hey, who are your pals?"

The two men were of medium size, athletic in bearing but without the marks of the pugilist. Café au lait in hue, they stood two paces to the rear of Coco staring up at Buchanan. Each held a carpetbag in hand. They were dressed in Eastern town clothing, very neat but worn. They looked watchful, tentative, as though they were present somewhat against their desires.

Coco said, "This one is Joe Mallet. The one with the squinchy eyes, he's Smack Keen. They been havin' a bit of trouble back East. Just like me."

"Uh-huh," said Buchanan. "Reckon we'd better set down some place and talk it over?"

"They got a cafe here takes black people in?"

"I got a friend here," Buchanan said.

"You lookin' scrumptious, Tom. You want to go a couple rounds with me later on?"

"I don't get into fights, even with you," said Buchanan sententiously. "Not unless they're forced onto me."

Sheriff Catlow said behind him, "But he do get forced. You boys all friends of Buchanan?"

"Any friend of Coco is a friend of mine," Buchanan told him. "You got those ballplayers locked up?"

"They'll be quiet till Masters turns them a-loose later on." Catlow squinted at the three blacks. "Got one rule hereabouts. Don't start nothin'. Anybody gives you trouble, come to me."

Buchanan added smoothly, "The Sheriff's color blind but some of the other folks are not. Let's go and eat some."

The stranger introduced as Joe Mallet said quietly, "Maybe we oughta get back on the train."

"No," said Coco. "I tole you it's better out here than New York. You better believe me."

"Same lawman, same cold stares," said Joe Mallet. "I don't see no difference."

"You're lookin' at the difference," Coco scolded, pointing at Buchanan. "And that Sheriff, he's a good man. Just so you don't start nothin'."

Mallet said sadly, "It don't matter who starts it, Coco. You know that."

"You follow us." Coco linked arms with Buchanan. They walked down the street to a small restaurant over which the sign bore the words "Widow Barstow, Eats."

Mrs. Barstow was a lean woman of forty, clean-featured, her hair hanging in braids down her shapely back. She came to greet Buchanan.

"Figured you'd be around. Longbo hollerin' for help, ain't he?"

Buchanan introduced the others, adding, "The

widow, here, she sees all, hears all, therefore thinks she knows all."

"What I don't know ain't worth listenin' to," she told them. "You-all set down. I got ham and sweet potatoes and corn and fixin's. That's all you can get. It ain't the fanciest but it's the best."

"In this burg it's the best," Buchanan agreed.

She glared, then grinned and went into the kitchen. There was an aperture in the wall, and the stove was not far from it. The widow had sensitive ears, Buchanan knew. He was on familiar ground here in Silver. He was never certain he could trust the woman. He had a notion that it was business first with Widow Barstow.

Coco Bean, the champion, his round brown eyes earnestly sad, was talking. "I chased that Irisher white champ all over the east. I challenged him in saloons and right at ringside. Nobody would put up a purse. They don't want no black man to wear that belt. I made a few bouts here and there for scoffin' money is all. Then I found these boys in New York. They was tryin' to get on a baseball team."

"Baseball?" Buchanan paused. "Okay go on."

"They the best, like I'm the best." Coco's head came high; he spoke with more emphasis. "Tom, they won't let 'em play. Cause they're black is why. So I told 'em, I said West is best."

"There's no organized baseball here."

"No, but there's jobs. Minin', anything. These boys got to eat."

"Railroadin'," said Buchanan. "You boys know about that?"

Joe Mallet, who seemed to be the spokesman, answered, "We worked the rails. Then the jobs give out back there." He indicated his companion. "Smack, there, he's the best batter in the world. He got to run an engine once."

"Accident," said Smack Keen. "Man got sick whilst I was firin'."

"You done it." Smack's lip curled. "They done paid you a dollah extry."

The husky man lapsed into silence. Mrs. Barstow and an Indian girl brought platters of food. For once Buchanan did not apply himself immediately to the fare. "So you went broke, eh, Coco?"

"Jest about had enough to get here. I told 'em you'd take care of us."

Buchanan gulped. "Uh-huh. Sure. We'll work it out."

But his money was invested for the most part in Longbo's Engine 69. He had known Coco for several years. They had met in an improvised jail in El Paso, from which they had escaped only to be entrapped by the Texas Rangers into a dangerous range war. Buchanan had become extremely fond of the fighter, a most peaceful citizen outside the squared circle. Coco feared and hated guns, but he was a handy man to have around under any circumstances. He was loyal and honest and true to his convictions and completely unafraid of anything that did not shoot.

Of course, there were others near and dear to Buchanan in the territory, such as Mr. and Mrs. Billy Buttons—and their baby. They had inherited the Mousetrap Mulligan gold mine. Buchanan would not call upon them; it was not in his character to take—he was a proud giver. Further, it was his fashion in life to meet all challenges. First the Longbo Mine, second the black men who needed his aid to get a new start.

"Baseball," he said again and then he began to eat with his customary gusto. To see Buchanan enjoy a meal was a sight indeed. He had missed a good many on the plains and in the mountains, and always he seemed to be making up for these deprivations. Coco's friends regarded him with amazement and respect as he plowed through two huge helpings of each viand provided by the Widow Barstow.

The day had turned hot and Sheriff Catlow was disgruntled, his feet on his desk. Buchanan sat across from him.

"You got those black boys settled?"

Buchanan said mildly, "They're men, and

they're in the hotel because I put 'em there."

"I know . . . I know."

"Coco's friends are baseball players," Buchanan said and waited.

Catlow's feet came down from the desk. "Ballplayers? Any good?"

"Coco says the best. Only the white people won't let 'em in the leagues back East."

Catlow's eyes were bright. "I got four good men. You know 'em: Lee Perry, Frog Foster, Pat Hogan, and Jack Lee. The town's hollerin' for a game. Masters wants a game. I recollect you was a ketcher some time ago."

"And Coco's got an arm you wouldn't believe. Him and me, we played catch for years whilst he was trainin' for a fight."

Catlow sighed in relief. "Masters has got a lot of power. He's got the best team in the West. At the least we might could give him a game."

"Uh-huh," said Buchanan. "My thoughts, exactly."

"He got them out of jail an hour ago."

"I'll see him." Buchanan regarded the Sheriff with care. "You run this town. Can you give my boys protection?"

"Hell, the town'll be with 'em," said Catlow. "Man like Masters, he ain't got friends. He's got people work for him, people scared of him, people crawlin' to him. But ain't nobody likes him."

"He'll bring in gunslingers if he thinks there's any chance him losin'.."

Catlow showed long yellow teeth in a wolfish grin. "There's where Mr. Masters ain't got anything on us."

"Could be," said Buchanan. He arose. "Might's well get it started."

"Mendoza at the general store's got them new-fangled gloves and bats and balls and things."

"I'll see Mendoza."

"You organize this and the town's yours. If by any chance you could win—the territory's yours."

Buchanan said, "I got what I want of this territory: The freedom to roam around. People like the Buttonses and Longbo and you. I'll be talkin' at you."

He went across the street. Colin Masters was seated on the verandah as before, smoking his thin cigar. Buchanan sat down beside him.

Masters said, "Two black ballplayers. Coco Bean . . . and yourself."

"The Widow does talk," said Buchanan.

Masters flicked ashes from the cheroot. "I don't like you, Buchanan."

"It's mutual," said he cheerfully.

"You're the sort of man I would never hire."

"You're the sort of jasper I'd never work for."

"Then that's established," Masters said without heat. "My players need a workout."

"And you want to make some kind of a bet."

"Any amount."

"Odds?"

"You name them."

Buchanan thought a minute. He had not yet deposited the draft to Longbo's account. He was tempted. On the other hand, he and Coco were rusty; the town players were ordinary in skills. He quickly added up his remaining available cash. "Five to one. A thousand dollars."

"Done and done." Masters was hugely pleased. "My men get the workout; I make a profit. A fine deal."

Buchanan said, "One condition."

Masters shrugged. "Name it."

"Sheriff Catlow umpires."

There was a moment's hesitation; a frown creased the brow of the millionaire. Then he said, "The umpire can't help you people."

"Also, Catlow's honest."

Masters nodded as though this was of no importance. "One week from today?"

"Right," said Buchanan. It seemed odd that Masters would give them time to practice. Yet they would sorely need the workouts.

"I will instruct my people at the bank to put up the money."

"Me too," said Buchanan.

Masters allowed himself a small smile. "It

will be a strange thing to do business with honest people. However."

Buchanan got up from the chair. "Trouble with men like you. Never do believe there's honest people around."

"An idiot could count them on his toes and fingers," said Masters.

"You hold that thought. It can be a lesson to you." Buchanan departed without further words.

Masters regarded the end of his cigar. Then he went to the telegraph office next door to the hotel. He wrote out a message. It was long and involved.

The clerk said, "This don't make sense, Mr. Masters."

Masters put down the money. "Just send it, my good fellow. Don't try to understand it."

On his way back to the hotel, Masters decoded the telegram to himself, chortling. "Send at once, thirty skilled railroad men led by Boss Boston. They come at night; they do not enter Silver. Further orders given here."

He prided himself on rising to occasions. It had not taken him five minutes to see his way clear, to know what had to be done—what had to be risked. But then he did own enough of the railroad to demand special cars at any time of the night.

He had conceived a huge distaste for Buchanan. The matter of the Longbo did not concern him. He would take it sooner or later, one way or another. Stone was a fool, ignorant of the ways of big business. The woman would come crawling. She would be forced to capitulate because she was an opportunist.

As to the girl, Adah, that would also be managed. Colin Masters had made a pledge to himself to bring both mother and daughter to their knees. To his knee.

Power, he thought, was everything. Because of his short stature they had made fun of him since he was a boy. He was physically underdeveloped in a land where muscle counted for much, where a Buchanan was a hero. Well, he had shown them. Buchanan was no more than a horsefly to be switched by a coarse tail, its life expectancy a mere twenty-four hours. He, Colin Masters, could make or break a hundred Buchanans at will.

3.

BUCHANAN walked down the street toward the bank, passing the Star Hotel where Billy the Kid had been employed when he was an honest youngster in his teens. The newspapers of the country had castigated the Kid, and the garbled history of the Lincoln County War had made of him a moronic, mean, back-shooting desperado. Buchanan had heard otherwise from old-timers and men not so old who had known young Henry McCarty—his real monicker—and his ill but comely mother, Mrs. Antrim. No one, they said, ever did know the real Billy, who died at twenty-two, shot from ambush in the dark by a man Buchanan had never admired, Pat Garrett.

But then there had been the character known as Wild Bill he thought, a fake as was Buffalo Bill, a couple of stagey men not of the breed which really conquered the West. And there was the Earp bunch, the brothers and Doc Holliday, of whom so many tales were told that no one could know the truth. Buchanan was a good friend of Luke Short, who was a friend to Wyatt, who was a friend to Holliday, and so it went, and you never did know the real inside of all people, men, women, and children.

Coco and the black ballplayers were resting from their jolting journey across country. The bank was down at the corner and across the street. The curbing of the new sidewalk was two steps high because of the danger of flash floods from the Black Range or the Mogollons or the other ranges which surrounded Silver City like guardians against the outside world. It was part of Buchanan's country; he was at home here as he was at Encinal, which was closer to the mountains and where his young friends the Buttons dwelt. Later he would visit them and his godson, their youngster. Right now the problem was Longbo—and Colin Masters.

As he stepped down to cross the street a man called, "Hey Buchanan."

He waited. He was known to many in this area, but this short, bowlegged individual seemed a stranger. He wore Levi's and scuffed boots, a faded blue shirt, and a good, if worn, Stetson. He had a thin, tanned countenance and a quick grin. He proffered a work-worn, surprisingly large hand and said, "I'm Lee Perry."

"Howdy, Lee Perry. Do I know you?"

"Almost." He flipped back his hat. He was sporting a fine black eye. "Them ballplayers knocked me out just afore you and Abe run 'em in."

"They seem like a mean crew."

"They right strong, you know? Ballplayers. Me, I work on the Cross J but when there's a ball game I get time off to play second base."

Buchanan said, "And you already heard about the game."

The grin widened. "You know the widder-woman."

"And she knows all."

"Dang if she don't. Nobody can figure how she does it. Course people talk in the eatery. But even so, it's downright strange how Miz Barstow gets in on everything."

Two wagons went by in opposite directions. People walked, some waving as both Buchanan and Perry responded.

Buchanan asked, "You want to play for us, is that it?"

"You know it!"

"Well, Abe'll have the say."

"He's a square-shootin' man, sheriff or no sheriff."

They crossed through the dust of Bullard Street. In front of the bank Perry squinted at Buchanan.

"You know old man Farraday's not here any more?"

"How come?"

"Change in the bank. They got a dude in there. From Frisco, the widder says. Anyhow, a dressed up dude. Me and Amanda Baker, we wanted to take up a little place. Gathered a few head and her paw was gonna help out. Farraday allus helped in such tights. Not this dude. Name of Bulfinch. Ain't that a bird?"

"It's a bird," said Buchanan.

"Yeah. Well, he's a bird."

Buchanan said, "You needin' help . . . I'll talk to Abe and we'll see what happens with the ball club and all. No promises, mind you."

"Amanda said she'd wait." The blue eyes wandered for a moment, then Perry said, "Sure pleased to meetcha, Buchanan. You mind the McCarty kid—Antrim—Billy the Kid?"

"I was just thinkin' about him, how people liked him hereabouts."

"May the good Lord rest him. Him and me, we was close when we were buttons. He had the sand, Buchanan. I hope I can have as much, makin' it for Amanda."

Buchanan shook hands again, an act he seldom inaugurated. "Talk to Abe about the ball game. Be seein' you later."

Everywhere he went there was someone, he thought. People needed a hand. Billy Button had needed it a few years back. Coco had needed it. There were others all the way a long path back on the frontier. If a hand couldn't be extended now and then, the hell with it, he thought, entering the bank. Maybe if Billy the Kid had strung along with honest Lee Perry he would not be dead up there in Lincoln County.

Maybe if someone had given him the right steer he would be a candidate for the ball team. It was and always had been a topsy-turvy world and now, inside the bank, nothing seemed changed excepting the people. They were all strangers. None looked like he belonged in Silver City. They had the stiffness, the thin necks, the pallidity of city folk.

There was new lettering on the door to the private office at the rear of the building, "R. W. Bulfinch, President."

A clerk stopped Buchanan with a flirt of his hand. "Have you an appointment?"

"Nope, just here on my own accord. Who gives out appointments?" asked Buchanan, looking down at his questioner, a thin man wearing eyeglasses.

"Mr. Bulfinch doesn't see anyone without an appointment."

Buchanan took out his bank draft. "Tell you the truth, I ain't dyin' of curiosity to see Mr. Bulfinch. Any bird can take care of my business."

"You wish to make a deposit?"

"To the account of Beauregard Stone, known as Longbo," explained Buchanan with care.

The man wet his lips. "Oh, I see. In that case, perhaps I should confer with Mr. Bulfinch."

Buchanan sighed. "I'll give you thirty seconds, son. I'm a busy man. Name of Buchanan."

"Yes, I see." The thin man beat a hasty retreat. "You are Mr. Buchanan." He fled into the private office.

Buchanan looked around at the other employees. They dropped their eyes to their work. It was very quiet in the bank. The air seemed stultified, hard to breathe.

The clerk reappeared. "Mr. Bulfinch will see you, sir."

"Awful damn good of him." Buchanan bent his head to get through the door of the private office.

Behind old Farraday's desk sat a willowy man dressed entirely in gray. He was balding and middle-aged. His mouth pursed, thin lips unsmiling.

"I am R. W. Bulfinch. Mr. Buchanan, I believe?"

"Didn't the little man tell you?"

"He did."

"Okay. Here's $8500 to be accredited to the account of Beauregard Stone. And you can make a draft for a thousand on the Encinal National Bank in my account. Send them a telegraph or somethin'; they know me over there."

Bulfinch accepted the draft. He turned it over and over, examining it as though looking for flaws.

Buchanan said, "When did Masters take over this here place?"

"Masters? I beg your pardon. The San Francisco Mortgage Company acquired this bank six months ago."

"You answered my question." Buchanan shook his head. "Either you ain't got the brains to sit in that chair or you know Masters controls the San Francisco Mortgage Company. Now just do as I ask, please. Time is a wastin'. Like Colin Masters sometimes says, 'Time is money'."

Bulfinch said, "This will take a day or so, you know. Clearance, authentication of signature, etcetera."

Buchanan had not seated himself. He now leaned his huge hands upon the desk. "Mr. Bulfinch, you do whatever you got to do. And you

don't have to even be polite. But you know
what I think?"

"I beg your pardon?"

"I think you're full of what we call bull skit-
tles. And I think Masters has given you some
orders about me. And I also think that if you
don't get your butt goin' and do like I ask
there'll be trouble you ain't lookin' for. You
understand."

Color mounted in the cheeks of the banker.
"I do not have to take insolence from you or
anyone else. I am here to do the business of this
bank in an orderly fashion. I intend to do so."

"Orderly is right. Make sure it's just that way.
I got to tell you, Mr. Bulfinch. I don't like the
cut of your brandin' iron. I don't like the way
you dress or the way you talk or the way you
act. Just do like I ask, that's all. Good day, Mr.
Bulfinch."

He left the bank, walking slowly, thinking of
how the country was going to hell in a stage-
coach wherever Colin Masters left his mark. He
walked over to the office of the Sheriff.

Coco and his two friends intercepted him.
Coco looked worried, his friends equally so.

"Sheriff sent for us," Coco said.

"Abe's all right. Don't fret," said Buchanan.

"Lawman calls, it ain't never all right," said
Coco. "Leads to shootin' off guns."

"Silver's not a gun-totin' town. Hadn't you noticed?"

"There's guns. I warned Joe and Smack, onliest thing about the West that's bad—guns."

"Which I've explained and explained," Buchanan said wearily. "Some day there won't be guns."

"Won't live to see it. Somewhere a bullet's got my name on it." Coco shivered. In the entire world the one thing he feared and hated was firearms.

Joe Mallet interposed, "Wouldn't know one end of a gun from another. But gimme one and I'll learn. They only scare me when the other fella's got one on him."

"Gimme a razor," said Smack Keen.

"You got a razor," Mallet told him. "Just don't let the white folks know what you can do with it."

Buchanan asked, "Shall we see what Abe wants?"

"He wanted *us*." Coco was not to be cheered.

They entered the office. It was a large room with a desk and chair and a bench and a straight-backed leather-seated pair of chairs and a rack of rifles locked against a wall. A door led to cells. There were spittoons on the wooden floor. Abe Catlow was scowling over a piece of paper, pencil stub gnawed down, poised.

He said, "Buchanan, we're short."

"That's what happens, a day late and a dollar short," said Buchanan cheerfully. "What are we short of, Sheriff?"

"A ballplayer." Catlow shook his head. "We got your three black boys, there. We got Lee Perry. Frog Foster, Jack Lee, and Pat Hogan, they'll do. We got you. We need one more. Town just ain't got anybody can play shortstop good."

Buchanan said, "Lemme see if I got it right. Coco pitches, I catch, right?"

"Right."

"Perry tells me he plays second base."

"Hogan's okay in left field. No more'n okay, but he can hit a ball a mile. Frog, he's a third baseman, not a youngster but always a ballplayer. Jack Lee, he plays the outfield good, hits pretty good."

Smack Keen said, "Respect and all, I'm a center fielder."

"The best," Coco said. "And Mallet plays first base."

"That fits in," said Catlow, nodding. "You got to remember, we're playin' professionals. Lot depends on pitchin' and catchin'. Mainly on hittin', though."

"How about speed?" asked Buchanan.

"You rode too many hosses to be a sprinter," Catlow told him. "Hogan, he's a blacksmith, runs like me—slow."

Coco said, "Me and my friends, we can run.

We done had to often enough."

Catlow looked at him. "Reckon so. Hereabouts, you run to me." He turned to Buchanan. "There'll be a crowd of people. I'll need deputies, since I'm to umpire. Masters has bought into things. Never know who's for what and who's against these days. Have to be real careful."

"Guns," muttered Coco.

"We got a gun law in this burg. Trouble is, so many people comin' in, can't enforce it a hundred percent," Catlow admitted.

"Odds are five to one. Will there be any local takers?" asked Buchanan.

"They hate those Westerners so, there'll be people puttin' up what they can afford. Some will get a load of redeye and bet more'n they should."

"Uh-huh," said Buchanan, "just like always."

"The Westerners ain't lost a game this year. Odds oughta be ten to one."

Joe Mallet said, "No."

"We only got a week to practice."

Mallet said, "Ain't no way the odds should be ten to one with us in the game. No way."

Smack Keen said, "Not if Coco can hold 'em."

"That remains to be seen," said Buchanan. "A week of hard work—we'll know where we stand."

"With eight players?" asked Catlow.

"About that, I got an idea," Buchanan told him.

"And practicin' here in town—that'd be a giveaway. Masters has got spies everywhere."

"And there's the Widow Barstow."

Catlow said, "Her tongue is hung in the middle and wags both ways."

"It's awful high up," mused Buchanan. "But if we can get used to the air, when we come down here it would seem a cinch to run, move around."

"You talkin' about the Longbo," said the Sheriff.

"I'll be goin' up thataway," Buchanan said. "I'll be findin' us a ballplayer."

"In the mountains?"

"I don't know any other place to look," he confessed. "Besides which, I got a couple little ideas."

"You goin' up there among them 'Paches?" asked Catlow.

"Me and Coco," said Buchanan. "Can you get the others to go up to the mine and start limberin' up? Tell Longbo I sent 'em?"

"Kin do."

"And tell him everything's okay at the bank?"

"I'll send the message, though I doubt it's the truth."

"Uh-huh," said Buchanan. "But he's nervish enough now."

"See what you mean," agreed Catlow. "Sure is hell when decent people have to kowtow to ornery bastards from Frisco."

"Or any place else." Buchanan tilted his hat. "Coco, your friends will be taken care of on the mountain. Let's you and me dicker for a hired nag and take a ride."

"You always ridin' me into somethin'," complained Coco. "Injuns or guns, one or t'other." But he grinned at his companions. "You go 'long with what Tom says. I'll see you up there —wherever that is."

"Just so it ain't heaven," said Mallet.

"No chance meetin' you there," snorted Coco. He followed Buchanan to the door, then paused. "What about them gloves and bats and balls and things?"

Catlow said, "The town'll provide 'em. Win, lose, or draw, the town backs its ball club. 'Bout the only thing folks get together with."

At the Bull's Eye Stable the owner brought out a dapple gray. "Good for the mountains. Stronger than he looks. He'll carry your friend."

"He ain't very big," Coco observed.

"Big enough," said Chambers. He looked at Buchanan. "We got any chance in this here ball game?"

"How should I know?"

"You bet on us."

"At five to one, hell, I'd bet the sun wouldn't rise tomorrow."

Chambers shook his head. "That ain't the way I heard it. You got somethin' up your sleeve."

"Don't bet your last pony on it."

"Wouldn't bet a worn horseshoe. Might bet a few hard dollars, though."

"On your head be it," Buchanan said. "Those Westerners never lose."

"There comes a time," said Chambers. He produced a saddle, bridle, and bit. "Need anything else?"

"Maybe a bedroll for Coco if you got one for hire."

"I got everything for hire." He grinned. "That is, everything not nailed down by that bastard Masters."

"He sure ain't a popular fella," said Buchanan. He led Nightshade out of his stall. The horse was always ready to go. They saddled up, the black champion and the frontiersman, and rode out of Silver City toward the Black Range.

"Sure wish we was goin' the other way, to Encinal," said Coco as they hit the first rising foothills. "Sure would like to see how that Button baby's growed."

"That's the next stop," promised Buchanan.

"After we get through here."

They rode to a clump of piñon trees. Coco started to go around but Buchanan held up a hand.

"We'll night-camp here."

"It ain't night, is it?"

"The sun goes down like a trout jumpin' a stream in these parts." The colors had changed in the hills and the afternoon was waning. "Besides, I want Vicenzio to know we're here."

"Vicen . . . who?"

"The boy I'm lookin' for."

"Like the man said, you lookin' for an Injun boy to play shortstop? Tom, you plumb lost your mind."

Buchanan dismounted and began loosening his gear. "Just take it from me. Vicenzio can cut it. If I can get him."

"How come?"

As they prepared the horses for the night and unpacked cold food from the saddlebags, Bucanan explained about Vicenzio. He ended, "The boy is torn between his loyalty to the tribe and a hankerin' to see what the white world is all about. Otherwise he wouldn't have stayed in school as long as he did."

"But the old folks can't make it without him —is that where it hangs?"

"That's about it." Buchanan sat down and rested his back against his saddle. "Look at those mountains. This is Apache country. They owned all they could hold of it against Kiowa, Comanche, Mexicano. Now the white men have driven them to the end of their world."

"Apaches, they're mean," declared Coco.

Buchanan was silent. Coco hunkered down and opened a package of bread and meat, chewed awhile. Then he said, "See what you mean. Black folks—they didn't have nothin' to start with in this country."

"The Indians did."

"Yup."

"So every once in a while they start a fight. Vicenzio has learned that they can't win. Still, there they are, his little tribe, all that's left of them."

"So they should be taken care of."

"Some of them will be. Some of them won't. Some will steal and get caught and killed."

Coco said, "You know what people say about you?"

"That I'm an Indian lover." Buchanan shook his head. "I've seen Indians as bad as any wild wolves. I've seen 'em as good as angels. And so have you. Color ain't it and you should know that about me."

"I knows it," said Coco softly. It was suddenly dusk. They ate and drank from canteens. It became chilly but they did not make a fire, instead donning extra clothing from the gear.

Coco said, "Them boys, Joe and Smack."

"Ballplayers."

"And thieves. They had to eat, like the Injuns. New York, that's worse'n any place out here. Crooks of any color you can name. You think they don't carry razors in their socks? They have to. They'd be long dead if they didn't. So I do see what you mean, Tom."

"But they can play baseball."

"You wait and see."

"I'll take your word. And what about yourself, back there trying to get a bout with John L. Sullivan?"

Coco shook his head. "I beat four black men and thanks to your friend the Senator got to fight Paddy Ryan."

"Sullivan won the title from Ryan."

"The police stopped our fight when I had Ryan hangin' onto the ground to keep from fallin' off," said Coco. "And then Sullivan, he began to duck me. Oh, it ain't him, John L. It's the people that run him and run the business. They don't want no black American champion."

Buchanan mused, "You're already the black champion. They just don't want you beatin' the white champion."

"That's what I meant. So . . . my friends and me, we come back here. Wasn't thinkin' of baseball."

Buchanan said, "Baseball is popular here.

There'll be leagues out here soon enough. Meantime, we get them Westerners."

Darkness fell like a kind velvet blanket. The odor of the piñons was strong and pleasant to the nostrils of Buchanan. He took a deep breath.

Coco rolled up in his blankets. Buchanan said to him, "Be sure and keep that right arm covered. You got to get it in shape to throw the ball over the plate."

"I'll throw it." Coco was already dozing.

Buchanan arose and walked the perimeter of the grove. The Apaches would be somewhere around, he knew. He would not be able to see them because of their wiles, but he could sense their presence. He knew this country and he knew the Indians.

Vicenzio had said the old ones could no longer lead. That was probably true, but they could scout an enemy. They could throw or shoot an arrow silently in the night and vanish like the wind. He had no desire to be a victim.

When he had come to the high point of the sloping foothill he squatted down and turned all his senses up to the fullest power. He sat for a long time, motionless as the mountains above him, silent as the grass crushed beneath his boots.

When the wraiths came silently beyond his vision but within his ken he spoke softly. "I am Buchanan. Tomorrow I will speak with

Vicenzio. With me is another friend. Do not cause trouble now. Know that I am ready for those who creep by night."

He waited. He heard a bird call which was not quite correct. He heard the coyote wail which came from a human throat. He read the sign, his mind going back to other times when he had hunted with—and against—the Apache. There was no spoken word in any language. In a few minutes he knew he was alone. Whoever they were, he had got through to them. They knew Vicenzio, the boy who had become a young brave and who was, it now appeared, truly a leader.

He went back to where Coco lay and wrapped the blanket around him and rested his head upon the saddle. He could sleep now. He was far safer than he would have been in town. Or in New York City, he thought sadly, thinking of the hard times Coco and his friends must have had.

In the morning he awakened before the sun. Coco still slept. Buchanan made a small fire and heated water for coffee. There was jerky and hardtack in the pack. It offended his appetite, but it would do until his business with Vicenzio was accomplished.

Coco came awake all at once, like a panther. He was running in circles, flexing his arms in an instant. He sniffed the air, slowed down.

"Smells mighty fine."

"Drink your coffee and save yourself. We got a climb ahead."

"They around last night?"

"They was around."

"You palaver with 'em?"

"A bit."

"Then they won't be shootin' at us?"

Buchanan said, "Hard to tell. They got troubles amongst themselves. But last night they went back to the place."

"What place?" Coco sipped the scalding coffee, made a face.

"The old place. White men ain't welcome there. But I been there before; they know me."

"This is real bad coffee," said Coco. "Let's get goin'."

They took the road known to Buchanan and the Apaches, to few others. It was hard on the horses but there was need for haste. Only one week lay ahead to organize and practice a ball team. Buchanan had experience in this work; he thought hard about it on the tortuous, often undiscernible trail upward.

The ball field at Silver City was a former flat meadow. There were aging wooden slats piled to make a sort of stand for the fans. Colin Masters was directing a crew of workmen, refurbishing everything in sight. Abe Catlow watched without expression.

Masters said, "I want my men to play under the best of conditions. We have a big game in Sacramento next week."

Catlow forebore comment.

Masters called, "That infield's level enough. Cut the grass in the outfield now, good and short."

Men obeyed him without question. They received their pay each night in hard silver if they satisfied the dapper little tycoon.

"Donlin!" commanded Masters. "Here."

The heavyset scar-faced man had bruises and a lump where Buchanan had hit him. He was the catcher for the Westerners and the captain by virtue of his ability to whip any man on the team.

"Here's the lineup. I'm switching Zale to shortstop and Leach to second. I think it'll work better."

Scar Donlin chewed tobacco, spit into the wind. "I doubt it, but you're the boss."

"We'll line up Leach, Gonzales, Bolto, McKale, Muller, Zale, Grogan, you, and Pierce. And I want Pierce sharp and fast for this game. I want these Silver City people shut out . . . humiliated. You understand?"

Donlin said, "Oh, sure. I understand, all right. Me, I want a crack at that Buchanan."

"There'll be none of that," said Masters sharply. "You want to catch bullets or baseballs?"

Donlin gestured at Catlow with a thumb. "Can't this two-bit cop keep order?"

"That'll cost you ten dollars," said Catlow.

"For what, tellin' you what you are?"

"Twenty," said the Sheriff.

Masters hauled out a roll of bills and handed over the required amount. He addressed his catcher. "One more word out of you and I take double out of your pay instead of the twenty."

Catlow pocketed the money. "It'll help buy stuff for our team," he said. He walked away, allowing himself a small grin.

Masters said, "In this town he is the boss, understand? I want no lawlessness. No more boozing. No more late hours. I want daily practice, morning and afternoon."

"For these hicks? We don't need it."

"You're going to get it," Masters told him. "Pierce started as an underhand pitcher. All right, he's good, but he needs to work on the overhand delivery. These new rules have made changes that demand practice."

"Aw, we could beat these amachoors with beanbags."

"I hope so. Otherwise, it is always possible that I could buy another ball team," Masters said coldly. "You do as I tell you. I have other things on my mind. I'm holding you responsible. And don't think you can get away with anything, Donlin."

"Okay. . . . Okay."

They knew they could not fool him. They knew he had spies everywhere. He had impressed it upon them from the start. He gave them leeway when there was no contest in prospect, but he yanked on the reins when the chips were down.

He strode to his shiny carriage, the one which traveled in a special box car wherever he went. It was driven by Callahan, his red-nosed hostler, and pulled by a pair of matched bays sleek as the owner himself. They went back to town, Masters lolling in the rear seat, one eye out for a good-looking girl who would respond to his wink.

He was very careful to wait for that response. He was far too canny to try it on a respectable female in a town like Silver City. He knew the consequences too well, wincing as he remembered a time in Colorado which he would much rather forget.

It was, he consoled himself, one of the very few defeats in his glorious career. A lady wearing the telltale flush of rouge waved a handkerchief at him from the walk, but she was a bit long in the tooth. He ignored her. He thought of

Adah. Vengeance upon Dolly but passion for Adah, he thought. Rather too bad Longbo, the oaf, had to be in the way. But a good thing to have a whack at Buchanan. He abhorred big men like Buchanan.

He ordered a stop at the telegraph office. He sent off several wires in his untranslatable code. He dismissed the carriage and went down to the hotel. The woman was waiting, wearing even more rouge. He sighed, then gave her an imperceptive nod. He went into the hotel and came out again. He slipped her a key and whispered, "Use the back entrance, please. I shall be with you in a jiffy."

He went into the bar and bought a bottle of the best whiskey. He had found that it helped in such situations. He could dream of Adah.

4.

ADAH slid out of bed and washed in cold water, her slim form shivering in the morning air of the high range. She was proud of her tanned face and arms, of the flatness of her stomach, the clean lines of her limbs. She had shaken the city ways, she thought—she was learning more every day about the countryside, the jagged peaks she climbed daily, the wondrous tall trees, the small animals that peered innocently at her from their native cover.

She donned men's clothing from the skin out, especially made for her by Mary, who had skill with a needle. The Levi's were boy size as were the boots she had broken in to fit her to perfection.

She slipped down the back stairs, going quickly past the room in which her mother snored. There had been another big fight the night before, mainly thanks to whiskey. Dolly had declared again her disbelief in Buchanan, had shrilled that he never meant to deposit the bank draft, that they would never see him again because he was a smart man and knew that Longbo was doomed. Nobody could stand against Colin Masters, she had said, and it had hurt Longbo, who did not deserve to be hurt.

Adah could only forget it all by exploring, getting away into the outdoors. It was, she had finally realized, part of the heritage which none knew about excepting her mother and herself.

Mary had breakfast and a cold lunch packed. "Knew you'd be goin' out. Sure and they shouldn't yowl so, the mither especial. The master was only defendin' his friend. He will be back, won't he, Miss Adah?"

"He'll be back." She ate with good appetite, took the lunch, patted Mary's pink, freckled cheek, and left the house. She made directly for a new path she had found, winding down from the mine, then rising, then dipping again through brush and a forest of pine. There seemed to be a sort of trail. She was learning about the different paths through what had at first seemed a tangled jungle. Animals made their way to water, to roots and other edibles, and she was fascinated with their innate, strong urge for survival. They stayed farther from the mine now, since operations had again been resumed, and if she went far enough her search was often rewarded.

She was walking with her head down when she became aware that she was not alone. She peered into the heavy thicket which was to the left of the narrow path. Two black, gleaming eyes stared back at her. She fumbled for the .32 revolver that Longbo had insisted upon her carrying in the hills.

A lean youth—taller than she, very handsome, red-skinned and muscular—stepped out and took her wrist in a gentle grasp. He wore leggings and a headband. He was an Apache, she knew.

"No," he said in good English, "I am not your enemy."

"Oh," she said, feeling suddenly futile and foolish, "I . . . I'm sorry."

"I am Vincenzio," he said. "I am friend of Buchanan."

"I am Adah," she responded. They continued to regard one another, now with growing curiosity.

"I have watched you often," he confessed. "You are walking an Apache path. You should not go much farther."

"Why not?"

"The old place." He pointed vaguely westward. "The old people there, they do not like White Eyes."

"White Eyes?"

He laughed. "The name they give you people."

"I see. We call you 'Indians' and that's not what you call yourselves."

"No, it is not. We are the People. Except that it doesn't translate exactly that way either, I learned at the mission school."

"You speak better English than I do," she blurted.

"I was thought to be a good student. Now, lately, I have spoken with no one but Buchanan."

"We expect him."

"He will come to the old place first." Vicenzio rubbed his brow. "I do not know how that comes clear to me, but I know it."

"Longbo—that is, Mr. Stone—says he is a great man."

"He is my friend. He has greatness."

"Well . . . I guess I'd better find another trail," she said. "I love walking in the mountains. I wouldn't want to intrude upon . . . upon—"

"The Apaches, who have been known to steal women and sell them into slavery in Mexico?"

"I've heard those stories." She was suddenly

78

defiant. "Is that in your mind?"

"Me, a mission school Injun?" he asked, mockingly.

"Well, you said you'd been . . . spying on me."

"Watching, not spying. Lest you run into danger." He bit his lip, as if wishing he had not made the statement.

"Then perhaps you've seen the other intruders. Those with dynamite."

"I have seen them."

"But you did not prevent them."

"How could I? And . . . why should I? You people have driven the game to cover, made our lives hard."

"Your people gave up this part of the mountain," she retorted.

"By treaty. White man's treaty."

She turned away, back from whence she had come. "It was nice to meet you. . . . What did you say your name is?"

"Vicenzio. We never speak our true names."

"I remember, now. In books they told about that."

"You will remember? Vicenzio?"

"I'll remember." She smiled tentatively. Then, seeing the look in his eyes, she flushed. "Maybe we'll meet again, here in the hills."

He did not answer nor make a move to prevent her going. She hesitated.

"Is there anything we could do for your people? I mean to make up for . . . chasing away the game you need?"

"Close the mine. Tear up the rails. Leave us to our own lives."

"I couldn't do that, you know. I can't do anything. I'm dependent upon the charity of Longbo Stone."

"Your stepfather is not a bad man," said Vicenzio. "The silver, it will bring other men, not good like him. It happened so with the copper. It will happen again."

Her face hardened, aged. "Colin Masters."

He said, "In school I heard of him."

"Buchanan may be able to help." She paused, then said, "If Colin Masters took over the mine —I would join the Apaches to fight him!"

He looked at her with curiosity. "You have fire."

"I know Colin Masters."

"Then work against him."

"How?"

"By aiding Buchanan," he said gravely.

"In any way," she told him with passion. "Given half a chance."

There was a bird call from above, beyond view. He listened, then answered in kind. He said to her, "I must go."

"Good-bye." It sounded wrong, somehow. She tried again. "Adios?"

"Adios," he said and smiled. "We will meet again."

In the flick of an eyelid he was gone into the brush. It seemed that she neither saw him nor heard him as he vanished. She stood a long moment thinking about the strange encounter. Then she walked in another direction, her head down, not looking so avidly for signs of nature's wonders. He was the handsomest young man she had ever seen. Nursing her own secret she wandered aimlessly that morning.

They had left the horses behind and were climbing. Coco was sweating gladly, thankful for the workout afoot. He said, "Anybody can hike up these here trails has got to be part goat. I mean regular-like."

"Apaches go where few white men can follow," Buchanan told him. "They're watching us right now."

"I don't see nobody."

"You won't. Not until they want to be seen." Buchanan was getting slightly out of breath. The last time he had ascended this trail he had been younger. He sighed, gulped another swallow of thin air, and went on.

They arrived at the old place, a perfect stronghold unassailable by attack, high in the side of the mountain. As they did, Vicenzio came loping from the direction of the Longbo Mine.

The older men stood against the stone walls, silent, disapproving. The young people raised their hands in welcome as Buchanan and Coco paused at the edge of the cliff, waiting for permission to go farther.

Vicenzio said, "You are welcome, Buchanan."

"This is Coco Bean, a friend," Buchanan said.

"Your friend is welcome."

An elder said something in Apache, half gestures.

Vicenzio replied, "The meat in that pot came from Buchanan. It is enough."

The communal pot was strung across a banked fire. A savory odor struck Buchanan's nostrils, and his stomach grumbled. Breakfast had been most unsatisfactory.

"There is more," he said, addressing them all, including the older women hanging back in the shadows. He took out his thinning pouch, making no secret that it was not well filled. He subtracted another gold coin. He extended it to the old man who had spoken. "For food."

The Apache turned his back. Vicenzio strode forward, accepted the money, gave it to a slim youth, and said, "You know what is needed. Take someone with you and go to the town."

The boy, expressionless, beckoned to one, then another of his companions. They were off down the trail in a moment or two.

Vicenzio asked, "And now, Buchanan, what is it you want from us?"

"Not from all of you. Just Vicenzio," Buchanan said.

"Speak."

"Baseball."

"Baseball?" Vicenzio's lip curled back. "I have done with that foolishment."

"A matter of money," Buchanan said, apologizing by shrugging his shoulders and spreading his palms. "Also, honor. Colin Masters stalks Silver City like a grizzly. He thinks to take all. It is to bring him down, to worry him, perhaps to defeat him in some way that we would beat his baseball team."

"And you need an Indian to do this?"

"Not any Indian. The boy who played catch with me and showed his great skills when he was at the school."

The brown eyes flickered for a moment. Then Vicenzio said contemptuously, "Have you seen the home team play?"

"Nope. Aim to try and improve 'em in a week."

"It would take longer. A year? Two years?"

"They're that bad, are they?" Buchanan shrugged. "Well, we got a couple of ringers. Coco brought 'em. Then we got him, you, and me."

Vicenzio looked at Coco. "He is the champion boxer. Baseball?"

"He's good enough."

Vicenzio showed slight hesitation, then said firmly, "I will not go to town and be made a fool."

"You think the Westerners can't be beat?"

"I think practicing with the Silver City men would be a disgrace."

No Indian would chance losing face excepting in a good cause, Buchanan knew. He said, "If we won, there would be an ample reward. Cash money. I guarantee it."

"And if you lose?"

"I would survive," Buchanan said cheerfully. He added, "But if Colin Masters takes over the Longbo Mine it will be hard with everybody."

"And the ball game has to do with taking over the mine?"

"Not exactly." Buchanan had to hedge. "But it may have some bearing." He did not quite see how this was true, but as always he was riding a hunch. Defeat would come hard to Masters, might send him fleeing in disgrace. It was a thin and dubious surmise but he clung to it. If Bo could get the mine working. . . . He concentrated on Vicenzio.

"We got eight men. We need you."

"You have, if what you say is correct, five men. The others are bad players."

Buchanan said in desperation, "And we're not goin' to practice in town."

"Where, then?"

"At the Longbo. There'll be plenty of food, and we'll have balls and bats and all that."

"At the mine?" It was the first sign of interest shown by the young Apache.

"Uh-huh. You can come home every night and see that things are okay here."

"At the mine." Vicenzio looked away, toward the Longbo.

"And I kinda thought maybe your young people could watch out for spies. Masters likes to use spies."

Vicenzio smiled. "You think like an Indian, Buchanan."

"Had to, many's the time," he said.

The old man who had spoken before now again let loose with a barrage of language. Vicenzio looked surprised.

"My father says you think well. He says you give food; therefore we should give help."

Buchanan raised a hand in gratitude toward the old brave.

Vicenzio actually chuckled. "He says the old folks can also watch out. He says they are better at that than we younger ones."

"He's probably right. Will you come then, to the mine?"

"You go there now?"

"Pronto."

Vicenzio said, "I will go."

"I will see you there. Adios."

Buchanan saluted them all, then led Coco back down the trail toward the horses. It was a stumbling, rock-scattering journey.

Coco said, "You left awful quick. I coulda used some of that stew."

"When you get what you want from an Indian—vamos before he can change his mind."

Coco said, "Seems to me he gave in pretty soon after you said we was goin' to work out at the mine. You think he's planning mischief maybe?"

They came to where Nightshade neighed impatience. Buchanan said, "Not after the old man spoke. You see, Vicenzio's pa is the real chief. Much as the Apaches have chiefs. They more or less have only war chiefs. But once the old one speaks they wouldn't go back on their word, not if you're a friend."

"I sure hope you're friend enough."

"I trust them a heap more than I would many a bunch of white people I've known," Buchanan said. "Let's get on to Longbo. That stew made me hungry, too."

They rode around and went up the trail now shining with the tracks that signified Longbo Stone's hope of the future.

When they arrived it was noontime and Mary

had the table laden with viands. Longbo shook hands with Coco and apologized for Dolly, saying that she had a headache. Adah came silently into the kitchen as was her wont and smiled at Buchanan as she joined them. For a while there was silence while Buchanan showed once more how much a hungry big man could eat. Mary watched him with adoring eyes, bringing him venison and potatoes and gravy each time his plate was half emptied.

Repleted, they repaired to the verandah. Buchanan recited the progress of their plans to Longbo and Adah. When he came to the part about Vicenzio the girl started, blushed.

She said, "I met him. On the trail to the old place."

"You've been to the old place?"

"Oh, no. He warned me."

"He's quite a boy, that Vicenzio," said Buchanan. "He comes from a strong line, from the great Mangus Colorado strain. Big men and strong."

"He's—uh—very good looking," she said demurely.

"No Injun is good lookin'," objected Longbo. "They all got that crazy straight black hair and black eyes."

Coco said, "Like us. Only we got kinky hair."

Longbo said, "Hey, I didn't mean nothin'. I

mean, it's the way things are. I mean . . ." He fumbled for words, was silent.

Buchanan said, "Just leave it lay there, Bo. You stepped in it; don't squash it."

Adah said, "He speaks very well, doesn't he?"

"Longbo? He speaks worse'n I do," said Buchanan.

She let it pass, looking out toward the mountain where she had encountered the Indian youth. There was the sound of horses as men came up the old trail along the railway tracks. Buchanan arose.

"By golly, that Catlow don't waste no time. This here is our ball team."

They had a wagon full of bundles and bedrolls, and the two black men were half crippled from riding up the mountain on livery hacks safe enough but badly gaited. Neither was a horseman.

Longbo went to meet them, long arms extended, all smiles, his open, friendly manner charming them. They responded in kind. The bowlegged Lee Perry was all grin. Pat Hogan proved to be a lanky young man with a long, drooping blond mustache—he was a blacksmith with bulging biceps. Old Frog Foster was squat and barrel-chested, as a third baseman should be. Jack Lee, the right fielder of the local team was young, good-looking.

Lee Perry said, "Reckon we got everything we need. Old Catlow come through good. No uniforms, though. Said we could all play in Levi's and blue work shirts he scrounged from the general store."

"Uniforms don't win ball games," Joe Mallet said. "Main thing is, we got a place to practice?"

Longbo waved an arm. "My men have been clearin' a space beyond the mine entrance there. Hope it's okay."

It was adequate. The trouble was, Buchanan thought, that it would take time for the men to get used to the rarefied air at the high altitude. The black men were already taking deep breaths, looking puzzled. He explained to them.

"When you get used to it, you'll be fine. And when you hit the ball it really flies."

"We got a whole box of balls," said Lee Perry proudly. "Golly, I seen games when we used maybe two for nine innings. They got so lopsided and dirty you couldn't see 'em, much less throw 'em straight."

Longbo said, "I got places for you-all to sleep in the extry quarters for the miners we'll be hirin' when the bank draft goes through and the engine's ours."

Lee Perry spoke to Buchanan. "We only got eight men, you know. Is Longbo goin' to play?"

Longbo laughed. "Lee, I ain't thrown as much

as a stone since I was ten. Never had one of them new brown gloves on my hand. Couldn't hit the side of a barn with a switch."

Buchanan interposed, "I've got the ninth man."

"Where is he, then?"

Buchanan winked at Adah. "At the old place."

"The old place? You're funnin' us."

He came down the path, swinging along, moving with no effort as though he was made of steel springs. He wore jeans and a store shirt which was obviously new. Buchanan jerked a careless thumb at him, making nothin big of it, as if it was perfectly normal for an Apache to join a group of white men with the intention of playing baseball.

"Some of you know Vicenzio. Might remember him from the school."

Lee Perry, youngest of the Silver City men, peered. "That's Vicenzio? Brother, has he growed."

At this moment Dolly came onto the verandah. She was dressed as for a party, her hair swept up and back. She swayed a bit but seemed in control of most of her faculties. She flashed teeth at Buchanan.

"I knew you'd come through, Tom." She caught sight of Vicenzio and uttered a small scream. "An Indian! That man's an Indian!"

Buchanan said, "And Coco is a black man, as are his friends. Let me introduce them, Mr. Mallet . . . Mrs. Stone. Mr. Keen . . . Mrs. Stone. And this young man, Mrs. Stone, is Vicenzio, my friend, a boy I taught to play baseball."

She drew herself up to her inconsiderable height. "Well, of course, any friends of Tom Buchanan . . . There is plenty of food in our kitchen. I hope you all . . . eat well, sleep well. And all that."

Her eyes fixed fearfully upon Vicenzio, she retreated, closing the door behind her. She had been into the booze early, Buchanan thought. That she should disdain people of color was funny indeed. She had unquestionably had to do with many in her San Francisco past. Sudden respectability did funny things to people, he concluded.

"Better get us organized," he said. The scene became one of activity as the men split up, deployed, unpacked, sought their sleeping quarters, then made for the kitchen. At least their welcome would be warm in there, Buchanan surmised, knowing Mary the happy Irish girl.

Vicenzio did not join the others. He stood apart, not smiling, not frowning, waiting. Buchanan went to him.

Vicenzio said, "There will be problems, no?"

"None," said Buchanan. "None I can't handle."

"Oh yes, there will be problems." He was not looking at Buchanan. He was looking at Adah.

Surprisingly, the shy girl came to them and held out her hand. "Welcome, Vicenzio."

Buchanan said, "Uh-huh. You two met in the hills."

"She complimented my English," Vicenzio said stiffly.

"He was very polite," Adah said. "Excuse me now. I must help Mary in the kitchen."

She walked away, graceful, lean, her head high. There was a difference in her today, Buchanan noted. He cocked his head and said quietly to Vicenzio, "See what you mean, bucko. There'll be trouble, all right."

Coco joined them. "Howdy, Vicenzio. Now we got our nine men, what next?"

"Everybody takes it easy for a day exceptin' me and Vicenzio. We're kinda used to high altitudes. We'll see the pitcher's mound is fifty feet from home plate and things like that there. Him and me, we got a lot to think on and talk about."

"There is more meat in the stew pot," Vicenzio said. "Therefore I am here."

"That's what you say. I half believe you," Buchanan told him, a twinkle in his eye. "The other half—don't try to fool an old ladies' man, son."

Vicenzio swallowed hard. He spoke with dignity. "I am Apache. You know me. Would I betray a friend?"

"Nope," said Buchanan. "Only . . . I'm your friend and the girl isn't anything to me."

"She is the daughter of your friend."

"Wrong again," said Buchanan. "She's the filly of that peculiar lady you seen on the verandah. C'mon, let's look over the ball field, such as it is."

Vicenzio was extremely happy to have the subject changed. They made their way to the level space prepared for them.

Mallet and Keen were unpacking the paraphernalia supplied by Catlow from the store in Silver City. They took out a strange contraption and handed it to Buchanan. It looked somewhat like a beekeeper's mask. There was a slit across it slightly above the middle.

"Some college kid invented it," said Mallet. "It's a mask for the catcher."

Buchanan removed his stetson and tried it on. "Hard to see much through it."

"Better'n a flat nose or a black eye," said Mallet. "You know the new rule. Catchin' a foul on the first bounce ain't out any more."

"You got the new rules?"

Mallet grinned. "You bet." He whipped out a

slim pamphlet. "Seven balls takes your base. No buntin' fair and then rolling the ball foul like they was doin' twistin' the bat. Pitchin' overhand or any t'other way is all right. Few little changes like that."

"Foul bounce ain't out," mused Buchanan. He took off the mask and regarded it. "Now if it wasn't for that fine mesh . . . Hey, we got a blacksmith." He examined the leather lining which protected the catcher's face. "And maybe we can make this so a fella could see what's goin' on."

Mallet produced a thin brown leather mitt. "This here is for you, too. You ever used one?"

"I can learn," said Buchanan.

Coco giggled. "Maybe you'll bust your right hand up and not be so tarnation quick with that pistol of yours."

"Thanks, friend," said Buchanan. "Let's get our food. There's a hungry bunch in there eatin' ahead of us." He thought about the mask, about his experience as a catcher when the ball had taken liberties with his face, coming swift off a foul shot by the hitter. The mask would allow him to get closer to the batter. A lot closer, he thought with satisfaction.

The baseball game was already taking on new aspects. The next thing to do was to find out how much talent there was among his players. It was something different managing a ball team. It was another challenge in a life which had faced a thousand of them.

5.

IT was midweek. The woman clutched a glass firmly in her right hand and said, "I know something about baseball. I saw it in San Francisco. If you think that bunch of misfit boobs can beat the Westerners you're loco, all of you."

They were in the drawing room, as she called it, Buchanan, Longbo, and Dolly. The men shrugged and were silent.

"We should be pushin' the bank," she went on, her voice shrill. "Gettin' that draft through. Movin' the ore down to the stamp mill. I tell you, Colin Masters don't spend time with his ballplayers. He's on the job every minute of the day and night."

"He's been on the job nights with Mabel

Potts," Longbo told her. "Miz Barstow's spreadin' the word so fast it got all the way up here."

"No matter." She swallowed two ounces of whiskey. She closed her eyes, seemed about to make another remark, changed her mind, finished the whiskey, held out the glass for more. Longbo lugubriously poured, one eye slanting toward Buchanan in apology

Buchanan said, "If I was you, I'd leave the worryin' to us. The banks'll be as slow as Masters wants 'em to be. Meantime Silver City is interested in the ball game, not in him. It's gripin' him some."

She said, "And that redskin makin' eyes at Adah. Now, that's got to stop."

Buchanan withdrew his attention. He had heard a noise outdoors. He came from his chair fast and went to a window looking out upon the front of the house. There was a general melee going on. He put down his glass and moved without unnecessary haste.

When he was on the verandah he saw that Coco had arrived. He paused to watch. There were four or five Indians involved. It was late afternoon and the ballplayers were running from their quarters toward the scene.

Coco began to sort out the combatants. His method was simple: He merely picked up the nearest and tossed him aside, then went for the next one. This man swung at him and Coco hit him in the body and sent him flying through the air. Buchanan came down the steps, picking up the victim, and examined him. It was a stranger.

Coco called, "I be a monkey's uncle, Tom. These here are girls."

Dragging the man he had collared, Buchanan went closer. There were two other rough-looking citizens. They were all wearing gun belts, but the holsters were empty. Four young people, all Indians, were now in a semicircle, beaming proudly.

A pretty girl said, "They spy. We bring 'em in, like Vicenzio say."

Vicenzio sprinted from the rear of the house. Behind him came Adah.

Buchanan said, "Spies, huh?" He peered at the three men, shoved his captive toward Coco.

"I think so." The pretty one was extremely happy with herself. "We trap them. Rabbit traps. They fell down. We pick guns from them."

Each of the girls held up a revolver. They shrilled a chorus of laughter. Vicenzio went among them like a lion. He seized the guns from them. He sputtered at them in their own language, waving his arms. They sobered, hung their heads, then trudged away toward the old place.

Coco said, "Hey, we didn't even thank 'em."

Vicenzio said sternly, "It is not fitting."

"Why not?" Buchanan drawled. "You start

these young-uns into doin' their own ways. Then when they do somethin' real fine you yell at 'em. To me, young fella, that ain't fittin'.'"

Vicenzio regarded him darkly. "You know, Buchanan. Of all people, you know." He stalked away with the guns.

Coco said, "They took guns from these fools. They brought 'em here under their own guns. Then they was fightin' em, without shootin' nor nothin'. I think they was hiyu gals, them Apaches."

"Uh-huh," said Buchanan. "But it ain't what they did in olden days. You see? Old place, old people; along comes Vicenzio, things fly apart. Even he can't get it real straight in his noggin."

Adah was gone. She had followed the Indian youth, Buchanan knew. He turned to look at the verandah. Dolly was glaring. Longbo looked confused. Buchanan sighed.

The baseball was bad enough. The local players were as bad as Vicenzio had prophesied. Colin Masters now had presented a problem— here were three spies, hangdog, bruised, and scared.

Buchanan asked, "You dudes got names?"

They muttered their names, "Cisco," "Jingles," "Cactus."

"I don't want to know any more about you— not even your real tags," Buchanan said. "Undo those cartridge belts."

They did as ordered. One asked, "You gonna let that damn Injun keep our guns?"

"Would you rather decorate one of these tall pines?" Buchanan asked them.

They lost some of their tan. They were cowboy types, probably sent in from one of Masters' many ranches to do the hard work of trekking through the mountains.

Coco said, "Mebbe I better push 'em around a little? Maybe it'd loosen them up."

They stepped back. They were wearing high-heeled riding boots in various stages of decomposition. Masters evidently did not overpay his cowhands.

Buchanan said, "They got troubles enough, I think. You boys lose your horses?"

"Them damn Injuns!" one of them burst forth.

"You must have got too close to their place. They figure any horseflesh ridden on their land is purely theirs." Buchanan shook his head. "Too bad. It's a long walk back down the trail."

"They'll be layin' for us!"

Buchanan said, "Do tell! And you without horses to ride away from 'em. Or guns to shoot 'em."

"You're not goin' to make us walk!"

"I am that," Buchanan told them. "You can have rifles. I would advise you to keep right on walkin'. Maybe to Texas. Because this story about you bein' hornswoggled by squaws—Masters ain't goin' to cotton to it, now, is he?"

"We didn't harm nobody."

"Didn't get the chance. The girls stopped you."

Coco laughed. In a moment everyone but the three spies was laughing, even Dolly Stone. A miner brought them rifles. They cringed, then turned and began their long walk down the trail. Ridicule, Buchanan knew, hurt them worse than could Coco, or bullets for that matter. They were outdoor types, proud in their own fashion. They would scatter to the four points of the compass, and none would reveal what had happened that day—and would deny it with violence if anyone dared to ask a question about Apache squaws in the Black Range.

Buchanan walked around the house in the direction he had seen taken by Vicenzio and Adah. It was late afternoon; the sun was flirting with the mountain peaks which towered above the mine property. He went behind the sleeping quarters of the miners and ball players and into a grove of tall pines.

The two young people were sitting on a fallen log. He came upon them cracking branches beneath his boots, making no attempt at secrecy. He sat down next to Adah and spoke to Vicenzio.

"I'll take the guns."

"I have hidden them."

"In case of what?"

Vicenzio said, "You saw the three men. There will be more of them. My people can use the guns."

"Your people don't need the guns. They just proved it."

"As I taught them."

Buchanan asked quietly, "And who taught you to make snares when you were a boy at the mission?"

Vicenzio said, "That is of no matter. They were able to catch those three men. You allowed them to go free."

"And you'd have killed them?"

Vicenzio started to make a vigorous assent. Then he looked at Adah and faltered. "You take the guns." He reached behind the log and took them from under dead leaves, handing them over one at a time, with reluctance. "I am only half Apache, thanks to you, Buchanan. But . . . the day may come when I regain my full heritage."

Buchanan collected the guns, stuck two in his belt, emptied the other into the sky. "Maybe. Maybe not. Meantime, there's this ball game. I don't know what Masters is up to. And you're right, we got some pretty bad players."

Adah spoke for the first time. "But not Vicenzio. Nor your friends. Nor you."

"Takes nine men," Buchanan told her. "They got nine."

He left them to their serious conversation, sorry that he had been forced to interrupt them. He took the guns into the house and put them in the rack. Longbo came into the room, a glass in his hand as usual. Dolly followed with the bottle.

Longbo said glumly, "Masters sure means business, sendin' three tough ones like that."

"Did you ever think Masters didn't mean business?"

"If only the bank would honor that draft we could start haulin' ore."

Buchanan asked curiously, "Why are you in such a rush, Bo?"

There was silence, broken finally when Dolly Stone poured herself her customary four fingers. Buchanan waited. He had sensed something wrong in the past few days—over and above the inefficiency of the town ball players.

Bo spoke. "Tell you the truth, some things went bad on the market. I had to borry on term notes."

Dolly said, "The damn fool. The notes are due in three weeks. Can you beat that? If we don't get rollin' in three weeks, we lose everything."

"Two weeks," Bo corrected her.

"And a damn ball game in between," said Dolly. "Grown men playin' games."

Buchanan asked, "You borrow this money before I got here with the draft?"

"Well . . . just a day or two," confessed Bo.

"Figured to get goin', get the note extended with the mine workin', everything would be all right. Now Masters is blockin' me."

Buchanan said, "Uh-huh. Well, now. You are what they call a cockeyed optimist, you know that, Bo?"

"Ain't you mad?" Dolly had lost some of her affected high-toned speech, it seemed. "Ain't you fit to be tied?"

"I ain't exactly proud and happy," said Buchanan. He stared at the rings on her fingers. "There's always a way out, look for it hard enough."

"Not my jewelry!" she said in a hard voice. "Not anything that belongs to me personal. You understand?"

"Oh, I understand." Buchanan arose. "Just was thinkin'. If Bo hadn't bought you so much junk he might not have had to borrow. Good evenin', folks."

She shouted after him. "And you keep that damn Injun boy away from my daughter, too."

Buchanan paused with a hand on the doorknob. "First off, I figure people take care of their own young-uns. Second, Vicenzio is a friend of mine, and he ain't never deceived me in anyway whatsoever. Third, I make it a practice of mindin' my own business."

He left without further words. He could hear her shrill voice, "Now you've gone and made

105

him mad at us. You and your dumb borrowin'
and fiddlin' around and not tellin' the man the
truth. And that Adah—she was always such a
good girl till you brought her up here. . . ."

Buchanan went out to the sleeping quarters
of the men. He had built himself a nook in that
building, preferring to sleep nearer the players,
to try and keep up their spirits, to be with Coco.
Once more he thanked whatever providence had
kept him from marrying. Many a time he had
been tempted but always the pull of the wild
country had prevented him. It was all roses
and romance at first, he thought, but once they
got a hold on a man he was through, finished.

With exceptions, of course. It never paid to
believe such a thing was absolutely true. The
Button family over in Encinal, now, and a
few others he had known were exceptions.

And even the good ones had their troubles
now and again. It was no life for Buchanan, that
was for sure.

The next morning they were early on the
improvised ball field. Buchanan knew no other
way to round his team into shape than to keep
them trying to overcome their mistakes. He had
the bat, and Coco had his leather glove. He
would hit the ball down the third base. The third
baseman would field it—sometimes, if it was
not too far from his chosen stance—and throw

to Joe Mallet at first base. Joe never missed any ball within eight feet of him.

Then Joe would relay the ball to Lee Perry at second base, who would toss it back to Frog, who would send it to Vicenzio. Vicenzio could be depended upon to get it back safe and sound to Coco.

In fact, when Buchanan hit the next one to the Indian youth's right, he backhanded it with the grace of a puma and rifled it straight into Mallet's glove.

Mallet growled, "At's the way to go, kid."

The next grounder would go to Perry at second base. At least twice out of three times it would fail to roll between his bowlegs. His throw to Mallet, however, was far from a rifle shot. He was slightly musclebound from wrangling broncs.

Anything hit to Mallet was gobbled up. Anything hit to the far reaches of the outfield where Smack Keen roamed centerfield—and a great section of both right and left fields—was also sure to be captured.

But fly balls sometimes struck big Pat Hogan on the head. Jack Lee had trouble finding them and often took them on the bounce.

Coco said, "We got part of a ball team, for sure. But it ain't the most part."

"It's five out of nine. Vicenzio is perfect."

"He can catch 'em. He can throw 'em. But

he don't hit 'em so good."

Buchanan said ruefully, "When I was teachin' him, we didn't have a place to bat. Nor a bat, neither, for that matter."

He called the team in. Coco would pitch batting practice. He would catch from twenty feet behind the hitter. They took turns, leaving their positions in order as he called to them. He hadn't the least idea how this was done professionally, he was making it up as he went along.

Most of them could connect with the easy throws Coco gave them. Where the ball was going they hadn't the least notion. Only the black men could really handle the heavy stick.

Vicenzio had trouble. He was slim and the bat was unwieldy, a virtual wagon tongue. Buchanan was struck with an idea. He left the field and went into the machine shop where the mining equipment was repaired and kept in order. He sought a piece of wood of proper length. He put it in a lathe and began turning it down. It was ash, he discovered, comparatively light. He worked on it for an hour.

He lifted it. Maybe it wasn't perfectly symmetrical but it would do, he hoped. He took it out to the field and called to Vicenzio.

"Try this," he suggested. "See if you can knock the ball out of the infield. Try and hit it where no one in defending."

Vicenzio scowled. "I can learn with the regular bat."

"Uh-huh," said Buchanan. "But we only got a few days. Maybe this will get you into it quicker."

Vicenzio went to the plate. Coco gave him a nice pitch over the center of the plate. Vicenzio swung. There was a satisfying splat of ball against wood. Perry dove for it, but the ball went on through to the outfield. The Indian youth was on first base before anyone got near it, kept going, and wound up on second.

Buchanan said, "Seems like a good notion, don't it?"

It was that kind of work all week, adjusting, experimenting, listening to the advice of the players from the East. Coco was working his arm into shape to deliver the ball with speed. He had a way of turning his wrist which was new to Buchanan. The ball seemed to change course in a curve.

Mallet said, "They're doin' that in the big leagues. It fools the batter a heap."

"Fools me, too," said Buchanan. "I got to know when he's goin' to throw it."

He was wearing the mask and squatting directly behind the hitter, now. It seemed a fine way to operate, but a lot of foul balls were nicking him here and there.

Mallet said, "You give him a signal. Like one

finger for a fast ball, two for a curve. Then you put your glove where you want him to throw it. It's simple."

"Nothin's simple," groaned Buchanan. He was getting hit in the chest by a lot of foul tips. His left hand was swelling because of Coco's strength and speed.

Mallet said, "Day of game, get yourself a steak."

"I intend to. A great big one, with mashed potatoes—"

"A raw steak. Stick it inside the glove."

Buchanan said, "Terrible waste of food. But it's a good idea, I reckon."

So they worked hard. Buchanan sympathized with the local men. The Westerners, undefeated, were awesome compared to Lee Perry and his friends. All hopes depended upon Coco and the professionals—and Buchanan.

It became Saturday, Buchanan stood outside the house that Bo built listening to the caterwauling within. He was dressed for town. He was wearing his six-gun, which was something he never did unless trouble was in prospect. He would turn it over to Catlow upon entering Silver City, but he wanted to know the polished butt and carefully oiled and loaded weapon was his for the asking. He was worried.

Longbo Stone came through the front door.

It was slammed behind him. He walked slowly to where Buchanan was standing.

"She's givin' me a fit," he said mournfully.

"Uh-huh, I could guess."

"I'm . . . I'm plumb sorry I didn't tell you about the due notes."

"You're reachin' for straws like any drownin' man," Buchanan told him kindly. "It don't make no matter."

"You'd have put up the money anyhow." Longbo sighed. "It's good to have a friend like you. It's hell to deceive him."

"You got troubles piled on troubles." Buchanan did not go into that matter more fully.

"She's yappin' about Adah. Chased me out to look for her. No way I can find Adah; she slips around here and there. Sure, she's with the Indian a lot. Can I stop her? She's free, white, and twenty."

"What about her real father?"

Longbo said, "Nobody knows nothin' about him. Name of Smith. He was some kind of soldier fella, seems like. Adah was born durin' the big war."

"She's a right nice girl. Ain't so shy since Vicenzio came to the mine," Buchanan said.

"Just what's worryin' her ma."

Buchanan changed the subject. "You couldn't bring Engine 69 down with the team? Get the townsfolk to yellin'?"

"I don't dare. If that bank draft comes through, I got to be able to move ore—pronto. Then the banks won't foreclose on me."

"Masters may think different."

"I got that money from friends that don't owe Masters nothin'," Longbo said emphatically. "It's their own necks they're worryin' about, not his —nor mine. They're good people, but business is business. That engine is everything."

Buchanan said, "Uh-huh. Good reason why a fella should stay out of it much as he can."

"I got you into this. And now this dumb ball game. You stand to lose on that, too, way I see it."

"Uh-huh," said Buchanan. "But it ain't over. I'm goin' down on Nightshade today and see what's doin'. You got a wagon there with good brakes. The team'll come down in it. How about you?"

"I'll be there." He hesitated. "Dolly plumb refused to have anything to do with it. She's got a bottle and . . . Well, that's the way she's carryin' on."

"Uh-huh." Buchanan had no intention of butting into any sort of marital strife. "Reckon I'll saddle up and go on into town."

"I got to look for that pesky gal."

Longbo took off for the woods. Buchanan went to the stable. Nightshade nickered, immediately conveying the message that they were not alone. The big black horse was sensitive in many ways; this was one of them.

Buchanan walked down the stalls of the lean-to barn. A roan horse was saddled; there was a murmur of voices.

He said, "Okay, it's only me."

Adah appeared, flushed, dressed in a smart, tight-fitting jacket, corded tight trousers, and boots. Behind her came Vicenzio, defiant.

Buchanan said, "Well, now. Reckon you're headed for town, girl."

"Mama is threatening to lock me up," she said.

"So you'll ride along with me."

"You wouldn't stop me?"

"Nope," said Buchanan, "wouldn't think of it. This here's the free-est part of a free country." He looked at Vicenzio. "You goin' by the old place before you come in?"

"I will ride in the wagon with the team. I will wear your uniform—clean Levi's and cotton shirt—and moccasins."

"You do that. I'm dependin' a lot on you. We all are."

Vicenzio said, "I do this for you, no one else. You understand that?"

"I savvy real good," said Buchanan.

"My people do not want this mine, these rails, this commotion."

"You already told me."

"He's right," said Adah. "We're depriving them of their very livelihood."

"Uh-huh," Buchanan repeated. "I know all that, too."

She said, "The baseball—he will show them that he can play their game. Then the truce is ended."

"Okay," said Buchanan. "You want to ride now, before old Bo accidentally stumbles on you two confabbin'?"

Vicenzio said with dignity, "We were talking of the problem of the Apache."

"I reckon. Sorta scared, ain't you? Not of people; you ain't afraid of people. Just of Adah, here."

Now she turned deep red. "He has no reason to be frightened of me!"

"Good. But right now, let's go down the mountain. Your ma ain't comin' so you can see the game and all. And Vicenzio, visit your people and hustle back, you hear?"

Vicenzio said, "You have been our friend. It shall be as you say."

Buchanan gave Adah a hand, and she mounted the horse. Nightshade was inclined to be a bit frisky, so that the girl was able to get out of sight of the house while Buchanan allowed the black his fun for a few moments. Then both were following the shining rails down toward Silver City.

After they had navigated the first turn and were slowly making their way down the steep grade, the girl spoke. "Why are you against Vicenzio staying to help his people?"

"Who said so?"

"He is no fool. He knows."

"Well, look at it this way: He ain't doin' much for them the way it is."

"He keeps the young people together. They survive."

"Just about," said Buchanan. "Vicenzio is one smart hombre. There was no one in the mission school near as good as him at readin', writin', and figurin'. And he could think. He could reason things out."

"And you wanted him to be a teacher?"

"That or something else. A lawyer, maybe. Like he could help his people in court."

"The courts of white men?"

He twisted in the saddle. The sun fell upon her aquiline features. Buchanan whistled.

"What is it?" she demanded.

"Nothin'. Nothin' at all," he answered. "Now you follow me around this sharp turn. Sometimes I get notions."

Nightshade was pirouetting just a bit, his head shaking the bridle so that it jangled. Buchanan dismounted. He removed the rifle from its boot. He removed his hat and went cautiously to the sharp edge—the same that had stood him in

115

good stead earlier when Vicenzio and his young people were destroying the railway. He placed his hat upon the barrel of the rifle and slowly thrust it into view.

A shot rang out, echoing in the canyons. He pulled back the hat, examining it. "Missed, by gum."

"Who can that be?"

"I don't know. But I reckon I coulda made a mistake."

"What kind of mistake?"

"Givin' guns to those three dudes we ran off, so's they could protect themselves against bears and what-not. I was pretty sure they wouldn't go back to town with their story. What I didn't figure is that they'd have the sand to lay for some of us."

Without fear she asked, "How do we get past them? Or do we go back for help?"

Buchanan looked at the cliff rising above the tracks. "Oh, we could go back. I could send you back, for that matter and hold 'em here. But I just realized how Vicenzio and his kids got down here."

"Down that cliff?"

"Look close. See the little depressions? They were dug by Vicenzio's ancestors. The Apaches always had a way to come and a way to go."

She said, "Climb the face of that cliff?"

"You ever heard of high gun?"

She shook her head. "I'm a city girl."

"Maybe you better learn." He grinned at her. "Seein' the interest you're showin' in Vicenzio."

She did not blush this time. She faced him and said, "You're right. I am interested in him. I think he's the most fascinating young man I ever met."

"Uh-huh," said Buchanan. "Wrangle your horse in behind Nightshade and trail the reins. Leave that little gun in your belt. Follow me."

It was precarious from the start. The handholds were tiny. It was harder for Buchanan's paws than for the slim fingers of the girl. They climbed. Amazingly, they came to a place of rest, a widening in the middle of the cliff. Buchanan hunkered there, putting the girl behind him. He stayed very still for a long moment. There was a flash of sunlight on a gun barrel across the gully from the old trail. He sighted, waited for a movement. Then he fired.

There was a wild cry. A body tumbled and crashed a hundred feet down to treetops, where it was impaled.

He looked at the girl. She was expressionless.

There was more movement in the brush across the way. He laid down a careful, low barrage. There was one more yell, then the sound of departing figures racing away from the scene of the ambush.

Buchanan said, "Hate to shoot a man. Purely hate it. They bring it on themselves. Still, it goes against my grain."

"He shot at us. He deserved it," she consoled him.

Again he regarded her closely. "You came up that mountain like a she-goat. And you a city girl."

"I . . . I don't know why. It seemed . . . easy."

"Your father's name was Smith?"

She shifted, a bit uncomfortable. Then she looked him in the eye. "That's what *she* says."

"You know better?"

"My father was the son of a mountain man," she said. "He was in the Army. Ma, she was young. I don't know if they were married."

"Smith?"

"That was his Army name. He was a loner, near as I can gather." She bit her lip.

"He was part Indian," said Buchanan.

"She taught me to be ashamed of it. Yes, he was an Indian. I don't know what tribe. He was the son of a squaw," she said. " 'Squaw man'— she said it like it was a disgrace."

"Who was the mountain men to marry?"

"I've thought about it. For years it's been something that I carried inside me. I'm glad to get it out."

"So Vicenzio, he's not an educated savage to you?"

"How could he be?"

"Does he know about your pa?"

"No. I . . . I can't tell him. It would seem forward."

Buchanan smiled at her. "That's a nice word. 'Forward.' Your ma sent you to a good school."

"She hasn't been all bad. Masters, he's bad."

"Uh-huh, he's plumb bad. Lotsa rich folks, they're downright peculiar. But he's worse'n most."

She leaned toward him. "Buchanan?"

"Yes, child?"

"I never was able to talk to anyone before. About . . . about my Indian blood. It feels so good."

"That's why you were so shy. Gettin' things out, it opens up people," he told her. "Now me, I'm Scottish. It's easy to say that on account of there's so many of us and we've taken the Indian country away. No reason to be proud. But there it is."

"You believe the Indians should get something back?"

"Lordy, girl, course I do." His face fell into seldom seen solemn lines. "I don't see how on earth they goin' to do it. But every time I get a chance I try to do some little old thing."

She said, "I've heard Bo talk a lot about you. Now I know why. He worships you. Oh, he fooled

119

you a bit and all that. But he thinks you're the best man he ever knew."

"That's real nice of him," said Buchanan. "Now, let's get back down to the horses. Follow me and be real careful. It's easier to go up than climb down."

It was not easy for him because of his bulk and because he had to watch the girl. Her feet were small and narrow and she used them well, but her hands were bruised by the serrated rock. They went very slowly, bold targets if one of the bushwhackers had remained behind.

Buchanan at last dropped the last eight feet and held out his arms. The angular girl was softer than he had anticipated. He put her down gently and examined her hands. There were no cuts and she could use her fingers.

"You're a heap stronger than you look," he told her.

" 'Courage riseth with occasion,' " she quoted.

"Riseth?"

"Shakespeare. *King John*," she said. "A good line, don't you think? It sticks in the mind."

He said, "I read some of that Shakespeare. Little Blue Books, they were. Got 'em with Bull Durham tobacco. Only I never smoked so I had to borrow 'em."

"Yes, Little Blue Books. I found one in the sleeping quarters when Mary and I were cleaning house. It happened to be *King John*. In school, they make you read the plays. When you're older you appreciate them."

They had mounted and were riding toward town. She was now an easy talker; all the shyness had vanished. It made a different person of her. She was bright and laughing and full of the wonder of life. Buchanan wondered if it was Vicenzio who had caused the personality-blossoming. Love, he thought, could work wonders.

The town was humming with bustling activity. Wagons thronged the streets so that they had trouble threading their way along Bullard. At the Widow Barstow's restaurant, Buchanan stopped.

"You go ahead in and eat. Listen, Adah, but don't say nothin'! Not a word. Just sorta nod and smile. Otherwise everyone in the Territory will know your business."

"I know." She smiled brightly at him. "Thank you—for everything."

"You're mighty welcome, lady." He touched his hat and led her horse to the stables of Jess Chambers. There was bunting, including a banner strung across the main stem; "Silver City Stars, Welcome, . . . On to Victory." Buchanan unsaddled Nightshade. Jess Chambers took care of Adah's mount.

"Had some trouble up there, didn't you?" asked Chambers.

"Not much."

"Three hard cases left without payin' me. Never did come back. Some say they was workin' for Masters."

"Do tell," said Buchanan. "You get a bet down?"

"Nope. Odds are now ten to one."

"Smart," said Buchanan. "Real smart of you."

"Ain't talkin', are you?"

Buchanan chewed on a straw extracted from a clean bale. "Way it is around here, silence is golden."

"Widder-woman says you got an Indian boy."

Buchanan was surprised. "How in tarnation did she find that out?"

"Couple of Apache kids came in with a gold coin to buy supplies. Masters saw that they got a pint. Well, you know what that does even to an Apache tongue."

"They got to braggin', huh?"

"Somewhat. Heard a bit of it, run 'em off to the old place. Still and all, town's a bit itchy. Indian boy—you know how people is."

"Ain't so crazy about it yourself, huh, Jess?"

Chambers spat. "You mind my brother Hoss? Sure, you do. Victorio got him up on his claim. Did some bad things to Hoss before they kilt him."

"I mind," said Buchanan. "You mind Mangus Colorado? How they flummoxed him, then murdered him?"

"I mind."

"Vicenzio is descended from Mangus."

Chambers spat again. "Mexican standoff, huh?"

"The country breeds it," Buchanan said soberly. "Let me tell you if it wasn't for Vicenzio and the black men, we wouldn't have a team to put on the field."

Chambers nodded. "Gotcha. Watch your step, Tom. There's a mint of money bet—people will take ten to one on a cockroach race, ya know. And Masters is actin' ugly. Like he's got a whole lot more'n baseball on his crooked mind."

"So have I," Buchanan assured him.

He threaded his way among the throngs on the walk, greeting old acquaintances, shrugging off questions about the game. He came to the bank just as it was closing, pushed his way past the pallid clerk, and went to the office of the president. Bulfinch looked up in great annoyance, then flinched as Buchanan loomed above him with hands on his desk.

"Those drafts I left here. Anything wrong with 'em?"

"Not that I know of. But there are processes through which they might pass."

"I could walk from here to Encinal and get it done."

"The mails . . ." Bulfinch stopped. "I'm sure they will be honored by Monday at the latest."

"Monday, huh. After the ball game."

"That's the best I can do for you."

Buchanan said, "The best, huh? Let me tell you one more thing. If they ain't all fixed by Monday I'm comin' after you. Not anyone else, Bulfinch. You!"

He walked out. He seldom uttered a threat and certainly none he did not intend to carry out, but the San Francisco banker had got under his skin. He went down to the Widow Barstow's place.

Adah was seated at a small table in a corner. He joined her, placing his hat on the floor. He had forgotten to turn his gun over so he unbelted it and placed it atop the hat.

Adah said, "There isn't a room to be had in town. And I didn't have to ask."

"I reckon. Well, Chambers has got a stable, maybe even a room in the house for you."

"The stable will do."

The Widow Barstow came past the crowded tables and stood, arms akimbo, grinning at them. "This gal never did talk much. Now she's gone deaf and dumb. How are you, Buchanan? No holes in you, I can see. You do in those three bad boys?"

"You got a large steak for me?"

"Steak? With this mob in town? Nix. I put every bit of beef I had into a pot and made stew."

"It's good stew," said Adah, dipping a spoon into her bowl.

The Widow said, "Catlow's been stackin' guns until it looks like a war's about to start. I see you still got yours, Tom. Worryin' about somethin'?"

"Only my stomach," he told her. "Biscuits, whatever you got, to sop up the slops."

"Slops? Why, you big, slab-sided, overgrown hunk of a maverick, don't you call my slops 'slops'."

She flounced off to the kitchen and was back immediately with an oversized bowl of steaming stew laden with succulent hunks of meat. "Eat that and complain, you big, fat, overstuffed saddle bum," she crowed. She slapped a platter of buttered biscuits on the table. "You want apple pie? A whole one, you hawg?"

"You sure are a wonderful lady," Buchanan told her. "Now run along and learn what you can and tell everybody all about it."

She laughed as she went. Buchanan laughed with her and ate, cleaning up both platters, polishing off the apple pie. Adah watched in wonder.

"And you're not fat, either," she said.

"Goes to my head instead of my middle," he explained. "You go to Jess Chambers, you hear? Stay there until I come for you."

"Yes, sir," she said, saluting.

Buchanan bundled the gun belt beneath his arm and went dodging across the street to Catlow's office. The Sheriff was sitting back, heels propped on his desk.

"You still got that hidey gun handy?" he asked, as he made out a receipt for Buchanan's Colt.

"Now, Abe, that's a personal question. I ain't *wearin'* a gun. That's what counts."

"I ain't splittin' hairs," said Catlow. "I got a cell full of weapons of all kinds. But I know there's twicet as many out there in the streets. I got ten deputies wanderin' around, half of them scared, the other half dumb. I'll have a few more at the game. Still, town's so riled up about Masters, anything could happen and prob'ly will."

"I heard of 'em yellin' to shoot the umpire," Buchanan. "Like if you make a mistake."

"I don't make mistakes. Otherwise I'd be dead long since."

"I believe you."

"Three gunslingers were seen talkin' to Masters. You had any trouble I should know about?"

"Not any I want to talk about."

"Masters has been sending gibberish over the wires. The clerk can't make head nor tail of them."

"Masters has got a lot of business here and there."

"Monkey business. There's somethin' in the air. Ain't you smelt it yet?"

"Right from the minute I rode into town," Buchanan told him. "But I can't place the smell."

"He's a smart one. Thing is, he ain't got this town treed nohow," said Catlow with pride. "Our people is, generally speakin', straight folks."

"Even the Widow fed me good."

"Hell, she don't have any other fun outside gabbin' her head off," said Catlow.

"The team'll be down in a wagon. You goin' to see they get through town okay?"

"Got the deputies all lined up for it."

Buchanan went to the door. "Angels could do no more. And you ain't even sproutin' a wing."

"More like a spiked tail." But the Sheriff was pleased. "I'll do what I can, fair and square."

"I know you will, Abe."

There were drunks in Bullard Street as it grew toward suppertime. Buchanan walked among them and spoke to those he knew, ignored those who staggered into him. He went up the steps of the hotel and asked for Masters.

The dapper little millionaire was in the dining room. His ball team was also there. They were eating steaks, Buchanan noted.

Masters said, "Ah, Buchanan. Ready for the slaughter?"

"Uh-huh. I'm ready for my bank drafts to be honored on Monday."

"Of course. You'll owe me a thousand."

"Uh-huh, so you say."

"By the way, three of my employees are missing. If I find you're responsible I will have the law on you, Buchanan. Not here. In Santa Fe."

"Now wouldn't that be somethin'—me responsible for anything like that? And a trial in Santa Fe?"

Masters said, "I may have more influence there than you imagine."

"With Governor Wallace? Why, I bet you haven't even read anything he wrote."

"Don't be a boor," said Masters contemptuously. "I take no back talk from ruffians like you."

The ballplayers guffawed. They were a tough-looking bunch. Buchanan surveyed them.

Then he said, "Give a man a bad name . . ." and picked up Masters' table, covered with food and bottles, and overturned it. Masters went down under the avalanche, his immaculate clothing splattered to the cuffs of his trousers. One of the ballplayers got up. Buchanan towered, facing them, legs apart.

"You want to play tomorrow?" he asked them. "If you do, just sit down and think kind thoughts."

They sat still. He walked out of the hotel and

down the street to the stables. He felt pretty good. If only he had faith in his ball team, now. . . .

Jess Chambers met him, agitated. "I got the gal safe in an upstairs room in the house. But my damn stable and half my grounds is overrun. By Indians!"

Buchanan looked past the livery stable owner. There were blanket rolls, unmistakably Apache, all over the place. One came toward him, smiling.

"We have come to see our son play the baseball," he said. "All of us."

Buchanan said, "Why, that's mighty fine of you. No guns, huh?"

"No guns. The Sheriff, he no like guns."

"Okay," said Buchanan. He turned to Chambers. "Whatever they cost you, put it on my bill. Might rustle them up some food. Send your stableboy down to the Widow, take whatever's left over."

"You goin' to pamper 'em?" complained Chambers. "Ain't it bad enough just to have 'em here?"

"They harmin' anyone or anything?"

"Well . . . no."

"Okay. Forget about your brother and remember Mangus Colorado for a night," Buchanan said.

He went into the house. Adah was rocking

in a chair beside a fireplace. Mrs. Chambers, a stout, benign lady, was crocheting across from her. They seemed comfortable and at ease with each other.

Buchanan went back to the stable. He took his bedroll from the shelf where he had left it and climbed a ladder into the loft. He wanted no part of the town that night. He wondered if Billy Button had come over from Encinal. He supposed that he had. The news would have gone all over, down to Deming, even to El Paso. The Westerners had a great following, and New Mexico had its pride. He rolled up on an opened bale of hay and put his head on a bag of oats. It was a better bed than he had slept on many and many a night.

Despite his worriment about the morrow he was off to sleep in a minute. He could always eat and sleep, which were enough for a man, he believed.

6.

BUCHANAN was up at dawn, washing himself in the horse trough, feeding Nightshade, thinking hard about the upcoming ball game. The town still slept off the hangovers from the previous night. He walked down to the Widow Barstow's eatery without waking anyone. Jess Chambers would see to the feeding of Adah and the Indians.

The Widow stood in the doorway of her place, waving her arms. Confronting her was a diminutive figure dressed in high-heeled boots, store-bought pants, and a bright-red shirt.

"This joint ain't open yet and that's final," she was yelling. "They kept me up all hours, and breakfast just ain't ready."

"Well, then, where's Tom Buchanan?" demanded the little man. "If the Sheriff's open and collectin' guns, why ain't the bloomin' town open?"

"Because too many loudmouths like you stayed up too late, sonny, that's why."

Buchanan arrived. "Thought you'd be around, Billy. Where's the wife and baby?"

Billy Button swung around. His face grew bright as the ascending sun. "Tom! Why didn't you let me in on all this? Damn it, I take a trip to Denver and all hell breaks loose in Silver City."

"Knew you'd either find out about it or else," Buchanan said. They embraced, Mexican fashion. Billy was married to the granddaughter of Mousetrap Mulligan, heir to a gold mine. He was a chesty little leading citizen of Encinal, a town near the Mogollons. He and his wife and baby were all the family Buchanan had in the world.

The Widow said, "Oh, Lordy, Buchanan and his friends." She stepped aside to allow them in and closed the door.

Billy said, "I go in my bank and the first thing I hear is you got drafts for ninety-five hundred. You been throwin' money away so fast and furious, that about cleans you out. What's goin' on besides a baseball game, Tom? You need anything?"

Buchanan nodded toward the window through which the Widow was listening to every word. "Nothin' much."

"Well, hell, this Colin Masters has been tryin' to take over the Encinal bank and now he's here. Tell me that don't mean nothin'?"

Buchanan sighed. "Maybe it does, maybe it don't."

"You don't want to talk to me about it?" Billy was very easily offended.

"Not right now. Let's eat first." Again he gestured at the window between the dining room and the kitchen.

The Widow Barstow called over the sizzling of frying eggs and bacon, "Don't pay him no never-mind, sonny. Just go on talkin'."

"She likes to hear all, tell all," Buchanan explained.

"Well, let her tell all that Billy Button is here and Tom Buchanan is good for anything I got."

The Widow called out, "And Colin Masters can buy and sell you and never miss the money."

"Now will you shut up?" Buchanan demanded.

Billy started to open his mouth, looked at Buchanan's stern visage, and shut it tight. Platters of food appeared, and the Widow opened the door and stragglers began to fill up the restaurant. Lee Perry came in with a wispy blond girl and brightened when he saw Buchanan.

"Hey, this is Amanda."

Buchanan and Billy got to their feet. She was a sweet, blue-eyed girl. They welcomed her and sat the two of them at the table.

Perry said, "I was hopin' to find you. Amanda ain't got anyone to set with. Thought maybe you could help out."

"There's a gal at the stables," Buchanan told them. "Adah Smith, stepdaughter of Bo Stone. You-all make sure to be early and set together."

"I'll be there," Billy promised. He was wearing a belt with a buckle resembling that of Buchanan's. He tapped it and nodded to them. "We'll be okay if anything starts up."

"There ain't supposed to be no guns," Amanda said fearfully. "Sheriff Catlow promised."

"Don't fret," Buchanan admonished her. "Sheriff's got everything in hand."

But he didn't of course, he thought privately. Nobody could, not on this day in this town.

In his room at the hotel, Colin Masters talked to Scar Donlin and a man dressed all in black who called himself "Keno."

"You get into the brush beyond center field. And stay out of sight."

Keno nodded. "I know what to do."

"He's the best damn rifle shot in the West," said Donlin.

"And you know baseball. You can keep score."

"Played some." Keno had a deep, raspy voice.

"Here's your money. I may need you later on for a movin' target or two."

Keno pocketed a pouch of clinking coins. "That's my business."

"He'd kill his ma for a hundred dollars," chuckled Donlin. "I know about Keno."

The man in black turned hard eyes on Donlin. "I'd kill *you* for makin' a remark like that."

"No offense meant," said Donlin hastily.

"None taken." Keno picked up a rifle that lay against his chair. "I'll be in position."

"You do that," said Masters. He watched the tall man pad silently out the door. When it had closed he shivered. "Moves like a puma, doesn't he?"

"Take away that gun and I'd hide him good," said Donlin resentfully.

"You attend to your part of this game," Masters told him. "Remember, Pierce has got seven balls before he gives up a walk. I want plenty of them thrown at heads."

"Where else?" Donlin was still sulking.

"I want Buchanan to look bad. Longbo Stone, I'm going to try to get a bet out of him. I've got him where I want him now, but a squeeze would do me some good."

"You sure don't leave no stones unturned, like they say."

"Unturned? I pick them up and heave them at people. That's the way to live. Just remember to obey orders and you'll enjoy some of the living."

"I'll remember."

Donlin left the room. Masters sat back and ran it all over in his mind. He had coppered every possible bet, he thought. There was no way he could lose. He must now search out Stone. If there was anything he loved it was tightening the noose around the neck of a man already, for all intents and purposes, hanged.

The firemen's band, bravely sweating in red flannel shirts, led the parade. The day was bright with the overhead sun, which would soon move westward to perform its wonders in reflecting the mountainside. The Silver City Stars rode in the wagon and people cheered.

Buchanan was at the ball park. He was checking the measurements of pitcher's mound, the bases, anywhere that chicanery could have been used. Sheriff Catlow had done a good job, he found, and the deputies in shiny, seldom used badges were in evidence as people began to jam the wooden stands and line up as far as the reaches of the outfield, beyond which was furze and brush so thick that a baseball hit there was seldom found. Buchanan sought Billy Button and found him in the stands with Adah and Amanda and Longbo. They were among friends, so that seemed to be all right. There were a hundred things on Buchanan's mind. He saw the Indians, grouped together, far down the left field line. They would know little of what took place; their eyes were only for Vicenzio.

The Westerners marched onto the field. They were wearing green and gold uniforms, the short pants and varicolored sox that were common in the eastern leagues. Their spikes shone in the reflection of the sunshine. They were long and cruel.

Sheriff Catlow spoke to Buchanan. "They might's well be wearin' rowels. You want to complain?"

Buchanan said, "Maybe they'll cut themselves. Let's get the damn game started."

The wagon had arrived. The players descended, stretching taut muscles. Masters came to Catlow and Buchanan.

"We are ready to begin."

"Not until my people loosen up," Buchanan told him.

Masters pulled out a watch. "One o'clock, that's the time we begin."

Buchanan looked at Catlow. The Sheriff produced an Elgin Engineer Special, nickel plated,

huge. "Ten minutes of one, Masters. You tryin'
to put one over?"

Master shrugged. "Must've set it wrong. However, take all the time you want if you feel that
way about it."

He went to where his men were gathered.
They immediately started to throw balls around
to each other, very tricky, showing off their
skills.

The Silver City Stars took the field. Buchanan used the heavy bat to hit grounders to
them in turn. They moved easily, none seeming
too worse for wear once they were in action.
Vicenzio's eyes darted to where the Apaches
had separated themselves from all others. Buchanan called to him, "They want to be together out yonder. Keep your eye on the ball."

Vicenzio hesitated, then nodded. The ball
went around, not with the fancy skill displayed
by the Westerners, but with increasing accuracy.

Catlow looked again at his watch, raised a
hand. He stalked out to the pitcher's mound
and yelled, "Time, gentlemen."

The Stars remained on the field in their various positions. The Westerners sat on a wooden
bench supported by two tree stumps and hol-
lered encouragement as Zach Leach, their third
baseman, took his place at bat.

Buchanan donned his homemade mask. Coco
stood with the ball in his hand. Leach stared

first at Coco, then at Buchanan.

"A nigger pitcher? And you a-settin' there in a face cage? You call this baseball?"

"Play!" demanded Catlow.

Coco promptly let fly with the ball. It came like a darting bullet, straight into Buchanan's grasp.

"Strike one!" roared Catlow.

"I wasn't ready," Leach screamed back at him.

Catlow merely stared at him. Buchanan remained close to home plate, crouching. Leach looked uncertain. Coco threw him another blue darter. He swung and connected.

The ball went down to Vicenzio. He scooped it up and threw to Joe Mallet. Leach was out by ten feet.

In his carriage, strategically placed where he could maintain close watch and the best view, Colin Masters grunted. "Speed. They've got speed, damn them."

He cast a glance out toward the brush far beyond the reaches of the outfield. There was no sign of Keno, but then Keno would have long been hanged if he had not had the ability to conceal himself while on a job. He leaned back, seeming to listen to sounds far away, pleasant sounds that brought a small smile to his face.

Tom Gonzales, the right fielder, was facing Coco. The pitcher swung his arm and threw.

The ball came swift and true, and Gonzales struck at it. Buchanan whirled, discarding the mask. It was a high foul pop near the stands. Buchanan ran under it, avoided the harsh sun and caught it in his huge hands. Two outs for the Westerners. The crowd roared.

Now came Kid Bolto, the speedy little center fielder. He held the bat high, shortening his grip, choking the wood.

Coco pitched the ball. Bolto turned, facing him, lowered the bat. Buchanan howled, "Bunt . . . Bunt!"

Bolto tipped the ball toward third base. Frog Foster came in on aging legs, picked it up cleanly enough—and threw it over Mallet's head and into the stands.

Bolto ran around, touching every base, turning to watch the progress of the ball. The fans had it and were tossing it back and forth amid gales of hoarse laughter.

Buchanan climbed over several people who shrank from his bulk and earnestness. A kid handed him the ball. Coco was at home plate, covering. Buchanan heaved the ball to him. Bolto slid head first and clutched at the plate.

"Safe," said Catlow.

Buchanan walked out and towered over Catlow. "You sure that's legal?"

Catlow said, "Nothin' in the rule agin it."

Mallet came over. "Ground rules. Ball's in the

stands—it's a two bagger." He pulled out the new book. "Right here, you see, man?"

Catlow scanned the book. Then he announced loudly, "Fella goes back to second base. No run."

Scar Donlin came swaggering. "Hey, what the hell is this?"

Mallet showed him the book. Donlin moved his lips, reading with difficulty. "We ain't had this here thing. Whereat you get this book?"

"From the man that wrote it," Mallet said. "You see here? Official."

Donlin said, "Aw, bullflop." But he sent Bolto back to second base and ordered Muggsy Mc-Kale, the left fielder, to the plate. "There better not be no tricks about this or the boss'll have you all skinned alive."

Buchanan said, "Is that where you got that scar? Did he start on you and quit?"

Donlin glared. "Just watch yourself, Buchanan, you and your face cage. We'll get you, rules or no rules."

Catlow said, "Play ball."

Everyone resumed position. Coco took the ball. He wound up and delivered his best fast one.

McKale, husky, mean, the best hitter of the Westerners, stood not upon ceremony. He slammed a grounder down toward second base. Bolto began to run.

Lee Perry committed the basic error of taking his eye off the ball as Bolto started. The screaming grounder went between his bowed legs.

Smack Keen came in from center field like a rabbit. He grabbed the ball and threw it to the cutoff man, Vicenzio, to hold McKale at first.

Bolto scored the first run of the game. Westerner supporters roared, and Masters sat back, lighting a cheroot, satisfied that all was well.

Buchanan called time and went to the mound, beckoning to the crestfallen Perry.

"Okay, a mistake. Coco, try turning it over, like when you were practicing. They're bangin' into your speed."

Perry said, "I'm so sorry I could bust a gut."

"Just keep your eye on the ball. Rule number one." Buchanan went back behind the plate. McKale roosted on first; Fritz Muller, the third baseman, was at bat.

Coco tried his new curve ball. Up until now he had thrown only hard fast strikes. This pitch was wild. He threw three more, all wild, making it four balls and no strikes. Sighing, Buchanan called for the fast one that Coco could control. It came low on the outside.

Muller hit it with all his might. It soared over the head of Hogan in left field. Smack Keen was running. McKale turned second and started for third. The ball tipped the glove of Hogan. By the time Keen picked it up and made a perfect throw, McKale was on third and Muller on second.

Boney Zale, the skinny shortstop, came to the plate. He was grinning from ear to ear. He held the bat on his shoulder, waggling a little, then returning it. Buchanan again called for the twisting ball, hoping Coco could control it.

It was a good pitch. Zale fouled it off.

He fouled off ten more good pitches in a row. This was his specialty. He could wear out the ordinary pitcher in one time at bat.

Coco, however, was not an ordinary man. As he worked, his speed and control improved. He came in with a fast one under the chin of Zale.

The shortstop swung around. The ball bounded down toward third. Frog Foster charged it. He misjudged the bounce. It went into left field. Vicenzio was over to grab it, but McKale had scored, Muller was on third, and Zale on first by the time he could throw in to Buchanan.

He held the ball. He thought for a moment, then realized he could do nothing about the ineptness of his local players. The Westerners could score runs. All that was left was to go ahead and hope his team could also score.

Coco rubbed his head. He did not complain about the errors. He accepted the ball from Buchanan and threw again. Biggy Grogan, the husky first baseman, let it go for a called strike.

143

Encouraged, Coco again threw straight and hard. Grogan, a mighty man, swung. The crack of the bat told the story. Buchanan watched the ball vanish into the brush, never to be found that day. The Westerners had five runs, all made after two were out. What had started so well was now a debacle. Scar Donlin was coming to the platter, laughing.

Buchanan again went out to talk to Coco. "These dudes murder your speed. Try some soft stuff on them."

"I ain't got much soft stuff," sighed Coco.

"Just keep throwin'. Someone may hit it to one of our good players."

Coco said, "Everybody hits. I'm doin' somethin' wrong."

"You're throwin' 'em too good," Buchanan suggested.

The Apaches, he noted, were stirring around as the younger people explained what was happening. They would be extremely unhappy. He wondered how many weapons were concealed among them. He wondered how many guns were in the crowd in the stands. It was not a pleasant situation. Too much money had been bet on the game.

Scar Donlin said to him as he went behind the plate, "You must have a yeller streak after all, wearin' that mask."

Buchanan answered, "Uh-huh, could be."

Then he gave the signal and Coco threw a soft, arching ball to the hitter.

Donlin leaned back. He swung mightily. The ball went straight up into the air. Buchanan ran forward three steps, waited. Donlin ran toward first. The ball came down. Buchanan squeezed it as though trying to strangle it.

The Westerners were out of the inning at last, with five runs to their credit. Out deep a boy scrawled the figure in chalk on a board. Buchanan gazed at it ruefully as his team came off the field. Then he scooted them all to the bench along the third base line, saying, "We got to get them back. Get up there and hit the ball."

Lee Perry said, "Gosh, I'd have to hit two homers to make up for what I did. I opened the gate for 'em."

"Don't look back. Look at here and now," Buchanan exhorted him.

The little man went to the plate. Pat Pierce, the Westerner pitcher, was a large man with a handlebar mustache and a fierce glare. He stared hard before he threw the ball, as though threatening mayhem upon the batter.

He pitched overhand. The ball went swift as an arrow, directly at the head of Perry.

The little cowboy went down in the dust. Scar Donlin laughed and said, "Get up, yeller belly, you ain't seen nothin' yet."

Perry got up. He dusted off his pants. He

stood in exactly as he had before. Again the ball came at him. He fell back, letting it go close to his belly.

"Ball two," said Catlow in a growl.

The stands were erupting with mingled rage and enjoyment, according to which side had been bet upon. On the bench Joe Mallet said, "Got to expect it and be ready for it."

"But how?"

"Pierce is first up next inning," Mallet said meaningfully. He winked at Coco.

Pierce now threw a ball a bit wide of the plate. Perry, happy to see something he could swing at, took a cut. He popped to Grogan at first. One out.

Smack Keen picked up the bat. He crouched as he faced the Westerner pitcher. Pierce hesitated, then again threw at the head. Keen stepped back and punched the ball. It went cleanly into right field. Keen ran to first as Gonzales relayed the ball into Leach at second.

Pat Hogan strode to the plate, an imposing figure bulging with the muscles of a smithy. Pierce threw him a tantalizing slow pitch. Grogan leaped at it and drove it high into the outfield. Bolto in centerfield caught it. Two outs.

Mallet was next. He looked at Pierce and laughed, shaking the bat. "Try to knock me down," he offered.

Pierce bared his teeth and said, "Try this,

nigger." He threw hard and fast at Mallet's ankles, an attempt to cripple. Mallet skipped aside, then swung his bat. As he did he let go of the handle.

"Duck, Sheriff," he shouted.

Catlow was already ducking. Pierce barely managed to fling himself out of the path of the missile. Mallet walked out to retrieve it, saying, "Oh, so sorry." When he got close to Pierce he whispered, "Try that again and I'll send a razor."

Pierce turned a bit pale. The batter resumed his position. Pierce took the ball from the catcher and looked at it, then at Keen, who was laughing quietly on first base. Then he wound up and delivered a fast ball on the outside corner of the plate.

Mallet did not seem to swing very hard. He caught it on the fat of the bat. It flew like a swallow, far, far beyond the reach of Bolto in center, one more for the tangle of the underbrush. Both runners circled the bases, and the Stars had two runs.

Colin Masters almost swallowed his cigar. He said to his coachman, "Go down and tell them to stop foolin' around and play ball. They can whip these clowns without throwing at anyone."

"Even Buchanan?"

" 'Specially Buchanan." Masters shuddered. "He might take it on himself to throw the bat at me."

The coachman trotted down on his errand. Pierce was pitching to Frog Foster. The aging third sacker swung behind three pitches and was out. The inning was over, with the visitors still ahead five runs to two.

The coachman came on the run to speak to Scar Donlin. The catcher scowled but nodded as he went to the bench and spoke to the other players. None of this escaped Buchanan as he knelt behind the plate. He gave Coco the sign.

Coco threw without windup. The ball came in like a bullet. It struck Pierce in the ribs before he could make a move. The pitcher went down in a heap, howling.

Buchanan straightened up. He tossed the ball to Coco, bent over Pierce, and asked gently, "Does it hurt, little fella?"

Pierce got to his knees, then to his feet. He clutched at the middle of his body. Donlin came out. Pierce said groaning, "He broke me ribs."

Donlin waved to his bench. A tall, lantern-jawed, tobacco-chewing player came in and picked up the bat. Donlin spoke to the umpire.

Catlow faced the crowd and announced, "Jingo Casey now batting for Pierce. The count is one ball, no strikes."

The new hurler stood back from the plate and indifferently watched Coco throw three perfect strikes, then went to the sidelines and began warming up to be ready to pitch the next inning.

Now it was Zack Leach again at bat for the visitors. Coco turned the ball over, and Leach hit it into the air between short and third. Vicenzio was over and under it, made the difficult catch with ease.

Coco was relaxed. He threw his swift one to Gonzales. He got two strikes on the right fielder. Then he tossed a slow one, and Gonzales swung and the pop fly came right back to Coco, who grabbed it. The side was out, one, two, three.

Donlin spoke to Buchanan, snarling. "Okay. No more chuckin' at nobody. Unnastand?"

"Why, I reckon it was just accidental," said Buchanan, wide-eyed. The town doctor had come from the stands to attend Pierce. They were calling for a wagon to take him to the hospital. "Too bad your fella got hurt."

"No more," Donlin repeated.

"Too bad. I was kinda countin' on havin' some fun," Buchanan told him. "But if you say so . . . all right."

Jingo Casey was unlike Pierce. He had mild blue eyes. He wound up like a pretzel. When and where the ball was coming from was anybody's guess. Jack Lee faced him and swung wildly at two pitches which were nowhere near the plate. Then he hit a weak grounder and was out.

Vicenzio took his light, homemade bat to the plate. The Apaches let out a mild yip, then were again silent. The pitcher threw a soft, curving ball. Vicenzio lit into it like an uncoiled rattler.

The ball went past Zale at short and into the outfield. Vicenzio was on first before McKale picked it up. When the left fielder momentarily fumbled, Vicenzio darted for second. The throw came in and the Indian boy slid around the short-stop—who took it—and kicked the bag with a moccasined foot.

"Safe!" declared Catlow.

"He was out!" howled Donlin. "Out by a mile!"

Catlow swung around so that his hand rested on the butt of his revolver. "You callin' me a liar?" he demanded.

Donlin inhaled, then went back behind the plate. Buchanan hefted the heavy stick and advanced to position. He looked at Donlin and asked, "Still the style to catch on the first bounce? I thought that was out of date."

Donlin growled, "You play your game, I'll play mine."

Buchanan addressed himself to the pitcher. He had never seen one who wound up in that fashion. He looked at a strike, then at three balls in succession. He let another strike go by, trying to fathom the style of the new hurler.

Casey threw a sneaky swift one. Buchanan finally took a cut at it. He hit it right on the nose.

Last seen, it was heading for that same distant brush, a home run.

Vicenzio trotted to the plate. Buchanan followed, not accustomed to running but happy enough to touch all bases.

The score was now five to four in favor of the Westerners. Coco had the big bat and was waggling it in his tremendous grip. Casey squinted, then threw seven straight balls. Coco walked to first base.

Now the Westerner pitcher moistened his fingers, then threw the ball. It took a funny, dropping course. Lee Perry hit over it. The grounder went to Zale at short, who threw to second to force Coco. Leach whipped the ball to Grogan for the double play, and the Stars were out for the second inning. Still, they had picked up two to be within a run of the visitors.

Buchanan went back to work. Coco pitched to Bolto, who again fouled off the ball a dozen times. Once it was a tip which smashed against Buchanan's mask, stunning him, making him happy for his self-made protection.

It was a tactic designed to wear out a horse, but Coco wasn't a horse, he was a man and a half. He took Buchanan's signal and turned his wrist. The ball came in spinning. Zale swung once more. The ball curved beyond the bat. Coco had his first strikeout of the game.

McKale was next. Buchanan stayed on his

toes, remembering the clever bunt in the first inning. Coco threw hard. It went for a called strike. Coco threw a curve. It was on the mark and McKale missed it.

Buchanan felt sudden confidence. Coco had found his control. He was smart enough to realize this and take advantage of it. He fed McKale a slow one. McKale knocked it straight to Mallet, who gobbled it up.

Now Muller was at bat. Coco turned his back on him, swung around, and threw another curve ball. Muller started to swing, tried to stop. The ball plopped over Buchanan's head.

Buchanan turned and leaped and reached out a long arm. He caught it. The Westerners had gone down in order again in the third inning, and the Stars were only one run behind.

Buchanan said to Smack Keen, "Let's get back that run."

The fleet center fielder grinned and went to bat. Jingo Casey threw him one on the outside corner. Smack hit it with all his might. It flew into the outfield. Kid Bolto made a terrific run and speared it for the out.

One more foot, thought Buchanan, and we'd have tied it up. He watched as Hogan hit a hard grounder but could not beat the throw to first. Then Mallet was up again.

Casey was very careful with Mallet. He threw six balls, keeping it away from the plate. Then he had to come over the plate. Mallet took his smooth, powerful swing. The ball sailed high. Buchanan, all the fans, all the players were on their feet. Kid Bolto ran fast toward the distant brush. The ball sailed over his head. It was another home run for Mallet, and the score was tied.

In the stands Adah was flushed, Amanda was jumping up and down, their natural shyness evaporated. Longbo came to Buchanan and screamed in his ear.

"We can beat them sons! We can whup 'em!"

Buchanan said, "It ain't over yet, Bo. Keep cool."

Casey outwardly cool, then struck out old Frog to end the inning. Buchanan went behind the plate. Within him a feeling was growing that this was not just a ball game with money bet upon it. There were other factors. He was warned by his sixth sense, which had kept him alive through the years. Something was brewing—he felt it in his bones—something serious and dangerous.

Boney Zale was up again. Buchanan sighed, expecting another barrage of foul balls. Instead, Zale bunted Coco's first pitch down the third base line. Again Frog was too slow. Zale beat it out for a hit.

Grogan came to bat. He took a ball, then a

strike. Then he also bunted toward third. The Westerners were exploiting a weakness they had found, Frog's inability to come in fast.

Buchanan flew out onto the field. Picking up the ball he threw hard to first. He got Grogan by a yard—but Zale was perched on second.

Scar Donlin took his usual walk to the plate. Coco threw him a hard one almost waist high. Donlin unloaded on it with all his strength.

Zale, seeing the direction of the ball over shortstop, began to run. Vicenzio leaped without bending his knees. He seemed to hang in the air, high above the ground. He speared the ball. He tossed it to Perry at second. It was a double play.

The Westerners could not for a moment believe it. Then they took the field, and their demeanor had altered. There was no scoffing. They were deadly serious.

Jack Lee was leadoff man. Buchanan said to him, "This pitcher is clever. Not as fast as Pierce —but smart. Watch his hand as he throws. He has tricks aplenty."

Lee nodded. He let four balls go by. Then Casey came in with two strikes. The next pitch was a floater. Lee bit at it. The grounder went to Zale, who threw him out.

Vicenzio went to the plate, and again the Apaches let out their single cry. Vicenzio struck hard against the first pitch. It rolled to Leach. Vicenzio almost beat the throw with his speed, but Catlow called him out.

Buchanan went to bat. He watched Casey's delivery with a careful eye. He saw the wrist turn over and looked for a curve ball. He got it as it broke and swung. He got a bit under the ball. In deep left field McKale made the catch. Three out and the score still tied at five all, and Buchanan was thoughtful. Both pitchers seemed to become better now, improving with each inning.

He was proven correct. Coco's speed became blinding; and his curve ball hit the corners or fooled the Westerners completely. The game was scoreless from the fourth through the seventh. The Westerners came up for the eighth.

Colin Masters was now uneasy. He shifted his position, again looking out far beyond the field to the brush. He lit a fresh cigar. His face was expressionless, but his hand trembled a bit. Then he shrugged, smiled to himself, and settled back.

Coco pitched to Casey to begin the eighth inning. He struck out the Westerner with ease. Leach came to bat. He had been hitless through the game.

Coco threw him the fast ball. Leach latched onto it. He sent it between second and third, nearly over the bag. Vicenzio flashed into the hole and made a fine stop, but Leach beat out his throw from the deep position.

Gonzales came up. Coco, watching Leach, who was fast, threw a curve that hung. Gonzales hit it into right field. Lee made a good return, but there were two men on base and one out. The dangerous Bolto was up next. Buchanan looked for the bunt.

It came, a good one, toward first base. Buchanan raced out and picked it up. His only play was on Bolto. He tossed him out as the runners advanced and the mighty McKale brought his bludgeon to the plate.

There was only one way to go, Buchanan knew. It all depended upon Coco. The first pitch was a ball. Then Coco threw his best fast ball, across the letters on the shirt of the big man. McKale got a good piece of it. The ball flew to center field. It was deep, but Buchanan thought Smack Keen could get it before it hit the deep brush. The center fielder ran back, got into position—and the ball vanished.

Instantly Buchanan knew it was impossible. It had been a sure out with Keen in the spot where he had awaited the descent of the ball. Yet here came the runners, three of them. McKale had a homer.

All the players and all the fans were stunned. Fritz Muller faced Coco. Buchanan's mind went around and around. Coco threw with renewed strength and fury. He struck out Muller. The score was eight to five for the Westerners.

Billy Button appeared. "Somebody shot that damn ball outa the air."

Smack Keen joined the group. "It was right in my mitts. Then it disappeared."

Buchanan nodded. "Masters with his ace up his sleeve. Can you get out there?"

Vicenzio, listening, said, "My people can."

"I'll ask 'em," said Billy.

Vicenzio wheeled around. He made hand signs. Young Apaches began moving, went from view.

Buchanan said, "You got your gun, Billy?"

"In my belt buckle."

"You and Longbo go the opposite way from the Apaches. Work slow and easy; the man's got a rifle."

Vicenzio said, "Let my people get in there first. They have weapons."

Buchanan said, "Take your time. There's another inning. Don't get caught."

It was a worriment, not about the game but about his friends and the Indians. Keen was leading off for the Stars; then Hogan and Mallet would come up. Three runs were a lot to make up, but these were the best men to try for it.

There were mutterings in the crowd but Casey

seemed unperturbed. Buchanan watched Longbo stop and borrow a revolver from one of his friends, then take off on a wide circle before approaching the far reaches of the brush.

Casey worked around Keen, finally got him to strike at a slow ball. It went sharply to Zale, who threw him out.

Hogan hit a high fly. McKale caught it. Mallet was the last chance in the eighth. He struck a mighty blow—and it went directly at Muller on third, who made a fine play to retire the side.

Coco went to the mound. Buchanan motioned him to take his time, to allow the Indians and Longbo and Billy to maneuver. Coco wasted a few pitches on Zale, then threw three straight strikes.

Grogan was next and Coco gave him the same tantalizing treatment. Grogan finally hit a weak pop foul, which Buchanan caught with his bare hand.

Scar Donlin was next. Buchanan wished he could reach out and swat the domineering catcher. Coco threw a couple of balls close, dallied, then came through with his speed undiminished, indeed increased, by the work of the day. Donlin, cursing, struck out to end the inning.

Now was the last chance for the Stars, and they had old Frog Foster, Jack Lee, Vicenzio to do the heroics. Neither Foster nor Lee had distinguished himself.

Buchanan pleaded with Frog, "Watch his right hand. He hasn't got speed, only control. Hit where he pitches. Just get on base."

Foster said, "I'll do my damnedest. There's somethin' damn rotten around here. I'd give a farm to beat these jaspers."

The veteran went to the plate. Casey began feeding him the changeups. Frog suddenly lashed out at one of them. The ball sped between third and short for a single.

Lee asked, "You want me to bunt?"

"Not unless you can run it out."

Lee said, "I ain't much but I can run."

He went to the plate. Casey fed him a low pitch. Lee bunted down the first base line and ran faster than he had ever before in his life. Donlin threw a bit high. Both Frog and Lee were safe.

Buchanan looked at Vicenzio. The Apache smiled gently. Buchanan said, "Hit it out, friend."

Vicenzio took his light bat to the plate. Casey worked the count to two strikes and three balls. Vicenzio, crouching, hit the next one. It went over second. Only fast work by Bolto and the slowness of Frog prevented a run from scoring. Vicenzio was on first.

Buchanan balanced the big bat. Three on base and his team three runs behind. He walked to the plate.

The crowd, caught up in mixed puzzlement and drama, was silent. Buchanan strained his ears but the tangled brush beyond the outfielders was too far, he thought, for sound to travel even in the light air of fifty-five hundred feet elevation.

Casey threw a strike; Buchanan took it. Casey threw two wide ones and a low one. Buchanan stood like a monolith, not stirring, bat ready, held high. Casey threw another ball. Buchanan tensed, believing the canny hurler would not try to fool him with a curve which would go for the third strike.

Casey delivered. It was as Buchanan had guessed. He could wait no longer. He put all of his might into the swing. The ball sailed in almost the same direction as had that of McKale which went for the home run. Foster lumbered home and waited, watching. Lee followed. Vicenzio touched home plate, then spun and ran like a deer for the outfield. The ball disappeared— into the brush. Buchanan made the tour of the bases. The game was over and the home team had won, nine runs to eight, as Buchanan followed Vicenzio.

Colin Masters spoke to his coachman. The horses wheeled around, and Masters was gone from the scene before the crowd could begin to believe what had happened.

Buchanan hit the outer limits of the field and crashed into the brush. There was a man lying at full length, dressed in black.

"Keno," said Buchanan. There was a neat hole in the man's forehead.

Longbo said, "He was turnin' on us. Billy got him with his little popgun."

Apaches were slipping through the tanglewood, going back to join their people. Billy said, "They come on him. He was lookin' up at the ball. They made a noise and he thought it was behind him, I reckon. He was easy, Tom, real easy. I was scared, but he was easy."

Longbo said, "Billy just nailed him in time."

"Thanks to the Injuns," Billy said.

Buchanan said, "Let him lay there. After dark we'll bury him. Otherwise there'd be a riot in Silver City, what with the booze and the bettin' and all."

Vicenzio agreed. "I will see to it that he is buried. Let the secret remain with him."

"Let's get back to town. There's money to collect and celebratin' to do with our players. And I want a word with Colin Masters."

But he did not find Masters in Silver City that

night. He collected the bet from Bulfinch. He paid off those he had promised. He drank some whiskey and pondered. Adah and Longbo stayed over, and Vicenzio did not return with his people to the high place until she had gone to bed. Everything seemed all right but Buchanan still had the feeling that things were not entirely in order. He sat late with Catlow, talking over old times.

The Sheriff finally said, "That feller who shot the ball out of the air. He was some kind of shot."

"He was," Buchanan said.

"He won't be no more," Catlow observed, tilting his drink, eyeing Buchanan.

"Who'll know?"

"Nobody." Catlow poured another drink. "You know, I couldn't stop the game and go see about it."

"It would've brought on a lot of bloodshed," said Buchanan.

"I figured you'd take care of it one way or the other," said Catlow.

"Thanks."

But Buchanan had his doubts. They rankled in his mind. Colin Masters was not one to accept defeat silently, to hie himself from the scene without comment. There was something rotten in the high country of New Mexico, and

Buchanan knew that Masters was responsible. He could not entirely enjoy the celebration. His thoughts were on the morrow.

7.

ADAH, Longbo, Coco, and the two black ball-players rode the wagon back up the trail. Buchanan on Nightshade went ahead, his mind still crumpled with worriment. The absence of Colin Masters meant something, of that he was certain. He wanted to talk with Vicenzio about the boy's future, but Vicenzio had evidently returned to his people. It was essential that the mine begin operating at once, sending down ore on cars pulled by the little Engine Number 69. Billy Button had returned to his wife and baby, and Buchanan wanted to visit with them, to rest for a while with Coco as companion on fishing and hunting trips. His muscles ached from the unaccustomed activity of the ball game.

He came to the last half mile leading to Longbo Mine. Nightshade pricked up his ears, a sure sign of trouble. Suddenly there were no rails. They had been torn up and carried away.

Nightshade increased his pace. There was an unearthly silence over the house, the quarters for the men.

And there was no sign of Engine Number 69. It had disappeared along with the rails. Buchanan dismounted and ran for the house.

The door was half open. He burst through and into the parlor, then the kitchen. He heard sounds from upstairs and mounted three at a time. Mary's Irish voice called, "Is it you, Mr. Buchanan?"

He found the bedroom door open. Mary was lying on the floor, tied hand and foot. He snapped open his Barlow and cut her loose.

"Where's Mrs. Stone?" he asked.

She chafed her wrists. "Sure and they took her along."

"Who took her?"

"A big, hairy man and a passel of 'em. Twenty, thirty, I don't know how many. They kilt one of the Mexicans and locked up the rest. Our bunch was too scairt to do anything. Them people have got guns."

"And tools," said Buchanan. "And knowledge of how to use the tools."

They went downstairs. Nothing in the house

had been damaged. Whoever had invaded the premises were not hoodlums. Colin Masters, of course, and his workers, Buchanan knew.

In the miner's quarters the Mexican laborers were completely cowed. They said there had been at least thirty of the men, they were skilled workers, they had quickly taken the engine apart.

"In pieces. Uh-huh," said Buchanan. They would not damage it. They would hold it until Longbo failed to deliver ore and defaulted on his notes at the bank. Then they would change the identifying numbers, reassemble it, and put it into operation after Masters took over. The ball game had provided them with the time to accomplish their mission. Immediately he knew he would have to find the hiding place and overcome a force of thirty men headed by the wily Masters—probably including in their strength the raffish ballplayers.

There was neither time nor purpose in calling for Sheriff Catlow. He would have to be notified, of course, but it was hugely more important to get to Vicenzio and the Apaches. He went to the kitchen and had Mary get to work providing cold food for an expedition.

Then he went out to await the wagon. Poor Longbo, he thought. It would be lucky if the shock of losing Dolly and his engine did not send him into a heart attack.

In the fastnesses of the mountains, atop a mesa, Colin Masters spoke to a short, wide, powerful man with intelligent features.

"Boston, you did a fine job."

"Only thing is, the Indians," said Boston. "They know these parts. They could find where we hid it."

"Buchanan could find it also," said Masters. "How many good guns do we have?"

"Plenty. They didn't like the hard work, but you gave me enough money to make it worth their while."

"The engine is not harmed?"

"Good as new when I put it together again."

Masters thought for a moment. Then he said, "There's only a few of the damn Apaches. Old people, young ones, babies."

Boston said sharply, "That's not my business, Mr. Masters."

"I know . . . I know. Who's your top gun?"

Boston said, "I don't like what you're thinking."

"Indians are killed every day. They stand in the path of progress. A few more won't make a dent in history," declaimed Masters.

Boston shook his head. "They killed a Mexican at the mine. I don't like it. I'm a mechanic, not a murderer."

"You do your job," said Masters soothingly.

"Just tell me who's the best gunslinger."

"Well, there's Keno," said Boston reluctantly. "But we haven't seen him around."

"You won't. The Indians took care of him. You see what I mean? They have to be eliminated."

Boston said, "Well, there's Corbin. He seems to be the leader."

"Send him to me at once," said Masters. "Buchanan will be on the trail."

He sat on a round rock. A ravine below was covered cleverly with swiftly planted underbrush, small trees. Boston and his men had done a good job of hiding the engine and the rails. It had cost a pretty penny, but the investment would pay off. It always did, for Colin Masters.

A tall, lean man came, rifle cradled, two revolvers tied low on his flanks. "Name of Corbin. Appreciate the pay. You got another job for us?"

"How many men have you?"

"A dozen good ones."

"You know where to find the Apaches in what they call 'the old place'?"

"Mebbe. Could look."

"You have anything against killing Indians?"

Corbin grinned. "Killed a heap. It never bothered my sleep any."

"You know a man named Buchanan?"

"Ev'body knows Buchanan."

169

"I want him killed on sight. I want the Apaches wiped out, no witnesses. I don't want the girl Adah harmed. Anyone else who gets in the way—you know what to do."

"Big job," said Corbin.

"A thousand dollars for each man who survives," said Masters.

"Makes it a smaller job."

"An extra thousand for you."

Corbin spat tobacco juice. "Makes it little enough."

"Pick your men and get started. Work fast. I only have a few days to complete this enterprise."

Corbin said, "Will do." He departed.

Masters got up from the rock and lit a cheroot. He walked around a small grove of piñons. Dolly Stone sat against a tree, her clothing disheveled, the rouge gone from her cheeks, looking all of her age. Masters sat down opposite her on a fallen log.

"Well, Dolly."

She said, "You're a bastard, Colin."

"So's your daughter," he said. "What of it?"

"Can't we make a deal?" she begged. "I can talk Longbo into anything."

"The time for talk is past."

"You're going to kill him?"

"Not necessarily. Only if he gets in the way before the notes are due."

"Let me go. I can handle him. I'll make him do anything you want him to do."

Masters considered the end of his cheroot. "You can also handle Buchanan, I expect?"

She slumped against the trunk of the tree. No further words would serve. She knew men. Now her only hope, she realized, was that Buchanan, whom she had so castigated, would know how to overcome Masters.

And no one ever got the best of Masters. In the end, he was always triumphant.

He was saying, "Of course good old Bo will do anything to save you, to protect you. Therefore, in the last ditch, you are my insurance. You see?"

She saw too well. She had been in many a tight spot in her life, but she knew this was the worst.

Buchanan was handing out arms to the leaders of the Mexican workmen. Longbo Stone fidgeted, waving his long arms. "They got Dolly," he repeated at intervals. "What are we goin' to do? They got my Dolly."

Buchanan said, "Everything in good time, Bo. Get ahold of yourself. I'm taking Coco and his men with me. You want to stay here or go along?"

Adah came from the house. Her revolver was strapped to her narrow waist. "I'm going with you. I know these hills. They can't have taken the engine too far."

"Vicenzio will know. We have to move fast, Sabbath or no Sabbath," Buchanan said. "Bo?"

"I got to go along," he moaned. "They might kill Dolly."

Buchanan took the tall man aside. "Bo, you got to get hold of yourself. There's a heap of work to be done and done damn quick. It's goin' to be ticklish no matter how we look at it."

"Masters would kill her in a minute if I didn't give in to him."

"Uh-huh. So we got to get her away from him. And to do this we got to find her. So you and Adah and Smack and Mallet, make two teams and spread out."

"How'll we know where you are?"

"You won't," said Buchanan. "But I'll know where you are."

"How?"

"Vicenzio," said Buchanan. "Now will you get goin'?"

He did not question the two ballplayers. He had come to recognize their worth. Smack went with Longbo. The bigger, stronger Mallet went with Adah. They started for the mountains.

"The valleys, the culverts, the ravines," Buchanan called after them. "Don't start a ruckus, now, until we catch up with you. Just keep watch. We'll be there."

Coco watched them go, then asked, "How come you know we'll be there, wherever 'there' is?"

"Vicenzio," said Buchanan again.

"I ain't too sure," mumbled Coco. He carried no weapon; he absolutely refused to do so. He depended upon his hammer fists and his agility to stay alive, even among the gunbearers of the frontier.

They toiled up the mountain at double speed. They came to the old place. The outpost waved them in this time. Vicenzio was standing against the wall of the canyon's ledge.

He wore a bandolier of cartridges. He was carefully examining a fine Winchester 73. He looked at Buchanan and shook his head.

"We are sufficient. I do not like the life of the town. We will manage well."

Buchanan said, "I need your help."

"Again?"

"Have you not been paid?" demanded Buchanan sternly. "Have I broken faith?"

Vicenzio said, "You are a friend. But I stay here."

Buchanan tried another tack. "Not for long. There's a passel of people with guns say you won't."

"We will fight them."

Buchanan said, "Not this bunch. They stole

173

the engine from the mine. There's thirty-forty of them, maybe."

Vicenzio shrugged. "What do we care for the mine?"

"They mean to take it over. Not harmless Mexican workers. Hardrock miners. Under Colin Masters. And you know the first thing they'll do? Right as of now?"

The old man, Vicenzio's father, stepped forth. "I am Nogalla," he said. He addressed his son. "Our friend is right. They will come here. I read the medicine in the city of silver. I saw it."

Buchanan said, "I saw somethin' like that myself. I didn't know what it was. But I felt it in my bones."

The old man looked at the sky. Clouds hovered around the towering mountain peaks. "You have shared with me. Trouble. Bad trouble is ahead."

Buchanan said, "I'd ask you to take the babies and women to the mine. There are guns. But they will not attack the mine. They've done that. They know the engine cannot be hidden from the Apache. They will come here."

"It is so," said Nogalla. "We will do as he says, my son."

Vicenzio seemed stunned. The older man had suddenly assumed dignity, authority not to be denied.

Nogalla went on, "The warriors will lead Buchanan. How many places can the engine be hidden?"

Buchanan added, "We'll watch them come here. When they find this empty, they will return. Then I must find the woman they have taken."

"The woman?" asked Vicenzio quickly, worriedly.

"The mother of Adah. Even now, Adah is out lookin' for her," said Buchanan. "She has only Mallet with her."

Vicenzio hefted the rifle. He waved to the young men. "We go."

It was amazing to see the Apaches break camp. In a matter of moments children and old men and young girls were going down the path which Buchanan and Coco had just ascended, their belongings in tow.

Vicenzio said, "You know which way the girl went?"

"Uh-huh," said Buchanan.

"We go."

Buchanan hesitated. It would have been better to remain in the vicinity and follow the Masters bunch. But he did not want to lose the services of the young Apache.

"Okay, follow me."

He led them down the trail. He had a vague notion which way Adah would lead Mallet. He knew her ways on the mountain trails. She would try to follow track. She was a city girl, but she had learned a lot. She was certainly intelligent. He plunged down the mountain and turned westward.

"They wouldn't go too far, carryin' that iron, with so little time," he said. "Vicenzio, what do you think?"

Vicenzio was doing everything but sniffing the trail. He was completely lost to anything else. He pointed and said, "There are men. That way."

Buchanan looked but even his remarkable vision revealed nothing to him. They were on a rise, the mountains towering above, undulating, densely covered wild growth in the direction indicated by Vicenzio.

He followed the Indian youth to cover. They shouldered through a thicket and came to a scattering of large boulders. Buchanan then saw the signs, the movement among trees. He said, "Take cover."

Vicenzio was already down and snaking along the ground. Coco dropped to all fours. Buchanan bent his bulk and moved from rock to rock, his rifle ready.

Vicenzio suddenly arose and emitted a curdling yell. A man showed himself, fired a shot. Vicenzio fired at him and missed with his new rifle. Buchanan shot the man in the chest. There was a wild scramble among the trees and the sound of men breaking branches to get to cover.

Buchanan said, "A little too quick, Vicenzio."

"You are right." He was crestfallen.

"Leave them be. We got other fish to fry." Buchanan began a retreat, circling always in the direction he had indicated to Adah, Mallet, Longbo, and Keen. They followed him, well spaced. Coco had learned much from Buchanan in their days together; he was able to keep pace and within hearing or within view of the others.

North of the mine Buchanan began a steep ascent. It took half an hour of hard climbing before he found the spot he had remembered. They rested a moment, looking down.

Buchanan said, "There," and pointed.

They could see Adah and Mallet, walking the edge of a canyon, peering down. They were sky-lined, an easy target.

"Go down," said Buchanan to Vicenzio. Then he altered his tone, saying harshly, "Lead them to where Masters is camped. But do nothing until you hear from me."

"Lead them to it?" asked Vicenzio innocently.

"You know where it is," Buchanan told him. "You know the few places it could be. You can reckon time. You know how long it would take them to reach a hiding place. Remember, they had thirty–forty men to hide the engine."

Vicenzio said obliquely, "You give me too much credit, Buchanan, but I will go."

"Watch over Adah and Mallet. Remember, they're city folk," Buchanan reminded him.

"I will remember." Vicenzio grinned briefly and began to work his way down the hillside.

Coco asked, "What we goin' to do now, just you and me?"

"Set awhile."

"Eat a samwhich?"

"Good notion," said Buchanan.

They broke out the food Mary had prepared and sat atop their high hill. Soon they could see and hear men working their way below them, going north.

"Reckon they buried their dead?" Buchanan asked.

"They didn't stay in the woods for long."

"Experienced gunfighters," Buchanan told him. "They couldn't find the Apaches. They were fired upon. They go back to headquarters."

"We follow 'em."

"Like I said."

"Vicenzio?"

"He'll take care of Adah," Buchanan prophesied. "He won't go off half-cocked again to prove his bravery."

"Is that what he was doin', yellin' and standin' up like that?"

"Uh-huh. Course he also wanted to try out his new gun. It carries a little to the left. He'll know it now."

"You and guns," said Coco. "One thing I do say, you sure fire know all about 'em."

Buchanan munched his sandwich. The last of the straggling band below paused, looked back. An unsuspected tracker would have run into trouble. They were experienced, all right. Now it was a question of finding the camp and extracting Dolly from harm. Then the fight could begin.

Not that he could really scrape up a whole heap of heartfelt alarm about the woman. She would sell out to save her skin, he judged. But he had come to this place to help his friend Longbo Stone. Marriage could really be a snare and a delusion, he thought. Love is often in the eye of the bemused. Nevertheless, it was Longbo's woman, and nothing would matter to the thin man if she was lost.

He said, "Well, we'll keep high gun on 'em and just mosey along."

They followed the range of foothills, slogging up and down, always keeping low. It was the toughest kind of going, since the enemy took the easy way. Still it was what Buchanan knew, what he, in his way, enjoyed: the use of his frontiersmanship.

Joe Mallet's razor flashed in the dappled sunlight of a glade. Adah swung around with her gun drawn.

Vicenzio said, "Excuse me. I should have called out, but there are men hereabouts."

Adah said, "Vicenzio, you came just in time. We're lost. We tried to follow track and failed."

"I know," he said gravely. "They dragged the trail when they thought of it."

"They have my mother."

"Yes, we must find them."

"But there are so many of them. An army."

"We will find them. Then we will await Buchanan."

Mallet said, "Yeah, Buchanan. Where's he at?"

Vicenzio waved toward the high country. "Up yonder. With Coco. He will know what to do."

"Have you seen Longbo and Keen?" asked Mallet.

"No, but we will meet them. It will all come together."

"And then?" asked Adah.

Vicenzio said, "Who knows?"

"Buchanan," Mallet repeated. "He'll know."

"No one is infallible," Adah said. "Not even Buchanan."

"True," Vicenzio said. "But until someone bigger and better comes to us, he will serve."

He led them toward the high hills. The going was uneven, but he knew the way. Adah, self-trained, kept close to him. Mallet, less fortunate but rugged, stayed a bit behind.

She said, "You were wonderful in the baseball game."

"A boy's pastime."

"But you were very good," she insisted.

"Buchanan was the hero," he said flatly.

"Without you, we couldn't have won."

"Thank you." He was silent, stopping, listening. Then he was off in a northerly direction, running at top speed, unlimbering the rifle.

Mallet, catching up, asked, "What you think he's after?"

"I don't know." She was already following as fast as she could. Mallet easily kept up with her.

Sounds came to them. There was a shout, then a shot. Adah redoubled her pace. Mallet reached into a pocket and brought out a snub-nosed revolver that no one had yet seen.

They burst onto the scene of the fight. Longbo and Keen had taken cover behind trees. Four men were attacking, closing in. Vicenzio's rifle spat fire. One of the men dropped.

Mallet said, "Outa my range." He moved, zigzagging. One of the men ran to fire at him. He flattened himself and aimed the little gun with care. The man fell down, arms wide. Vicenzio threw another shot. Longbo and Keen peered, saw nothing, went back to cover. The two remaining Masters people turned and ran. Vicenzio coolly shot one in the back.

"Good," said Adah, surprising herself. "Every man we get is one less to fight later."

Vicenzio said, "I thought you were a city girl."

"That time is gone."

He looked long at her. "Is it? Wait until this is over. What you will see may send you back to the city."

"Never," she declared. "I have found my life."

He started to speak, stopped. Longbo and Keen were advancing. Mallet reloaded the chamber of his little gun.

Keen said, "I thought you left that in New York."

"Couldn't bring myself to part with it," said Mallet, grinning. "Used it a couple times back there, thought it might come in handy someday."

Vicenzio was scouting the place where the enemy had fallen. Longbo, haggard, came to Adah.

"Does he know? I've been scared to do most anything for fear they'd take it out on Dolly. They might've killed us if you hadn't come along."

"You have to pull yourself together, Bo," she said kindly. "Vicenzio will lead us to Buchanan. Then we'll know."

"Maybe. Colin Masters, he's so damn smart."

"You're quitting before you know the answer," she said sharply.

"I know. . . . I know . . . I want her back safe."

Adah suggested, "If you don't get the mine affairs cleared up, Bo, what good would it do?"

He flinched. "I dunno, Adah girl. I just don't know."

Vicenzio returned. He seemed to bristle with weapons. He handed a rifle to Adah, one to Mallet. He gave a revolver to Keen and stuck one in his belt. He was still wearing the Levi's and shirt from the ball game. He seemed to have aged somehow; there were hard lines around his mouth.

He said, "We will go north. No use to separate again."

"You know where they are?" asked Longbo.

"One of two places." He paused, then said, "One of those people lived a few moments."

"Oh," said Adah. Then she said, "You lead the way."

Had he tortured the man to get information? she wondered. There were depths to this young man which she feared at this time to explore, to even think about. She followed him in the direction he indicated.

Buchanan and Coco sat on a high peak. The wind blew and they shivered. Buchanan was watching the last of the stragglers who were returning to Masters' camp.

Coco said, "We got to think of somethin'."

"Like where is Longbo and the girl and Vicenzio."

"Where's they?"

"Alive, I hope. You heard the gunshots."

Coco brooded, "Guns, always guns."

"I hope they were ours." He leaped to his feet. "There!"

"Where?"

"Down by that stream." He started down the side of the precipitous peak. Coco followed, agile as a mountain goat. They came to a thickly wooded section of a ravine.

Buchanan called loudly, "Vicenzio!"

The reply was instant. In a few moments they were together. Buchanan looked them over.

"I see you won the battle."

"But not the war," said Vicenzio. "Do you know where they are?"

"Just about."

Longbo said, "We can't do nothin' much. They'll kill Dolly."

"They won't kill her until they've talked," Buchanan assured him. "Thing is, if we confab with 'em they got her as the ace."

Vicenzio said, "There are ways."

"No," replied Buchanan. "There's no way but one."

Vicenzio shrugged. "If you say so."

"I'm goin' in soon as we're sure."

Vicenzio said, "Should we scout, you and I?"

Buchanan looked at the remainder of the group. "Reckon you'd better bring up the rear guard. Be real careful. Move slow. You think you know, huh?"

"I looked from a tall tree. There is a gully missing," said Vicenzio.

"The one near the giant firs?"

"That one."

"Then they buried the engine. Figured we wouldn't be onto them so quick."

"Just so," said Vicenzio.

"We got daylight. I'll move around. When I locate their camp we'll see what happens."

Vicenzio asked, "And if you get killed?"

Adah gasped, but Buchanan merely grinned. "Then you'll have to take over."

"An Indian leading white folks?"

Coco said, "What you mean, white folks? I only see two besides Tom."

"It was a joke," said Vicenzio lamely. "Buchanan understands."

"It was a dumb joke," said Buchanan. "I'll be taking off. You people just do what Vicenzio says."

"You got to save Dolly," Longbo pled.

"Uh-huh," acknowledged Buchanan.

"You just got to, Tom. Can't I go along?"

"Shakin' the way you are? You been in the cities too long, Bo. You stay and wait."

He left his rifle behind. It would hamper him, he thought, on the errand which he was undertaking—and for which he had no great stomach. He remembered that he was hungry and searched for another sandwich as he went in among the trees and disappeared from view of the others.

Adah said, "Which way do we go?"

"We wait," Vicenzio said.

"Wait?" demanded Longbo. "I say we should sashay up to wherever that bastard has got Dolly. and then wait."

Vicenzio was silent.

Adah said, "You heard Buchanan: Vicenzio leads; we follow."

"I swear, I don't understand you nohow," muttered Longbo. "You ain't like you used to be, none at all."

"You're right," she told him. "Maybe we should all eat something. We'll need strength for what's ahead."

She sat beside the Indian youth as they ate their cold food. He was silent and somewhat aloof. She was puzzled.

"Don't you want to talk with me?" she asked.

"I am afraid to talk to you."

"I thought we were friends."

"You are not like our women."

"Of course not. How could I be?"

"Yet you do not fear."

"I've been afraid many times in my life.

When I came to the mountains I began to see life differently. It was like a door had opened for me."

"The mountains. It was all ours, all this land, the copper, the silver. And the Apaches did not know how to work it."

"They could learn. You could teach them."

"I do not know," he confessed. "I have not the experience."

"You could learn."

"It is too late."

She said earnestly, "It wasn't too late for me to learn about the mountains. About you."

"You know nothing of me."

She said boldly, "Maybe I know enough."

He stared at her. She did not flinch.

Longbo interrupted querulously, "We got to get goin'. We got to meet Buchanan somewhere. Vicenzio?"

"Yes. We will meet Buchanan." The girl reached out her hand, and he helped her to her feet. For a moment they stood, hands clasped. Then Vicenzio led them to the next steep hill over which they must make their slow way.

8.

BUCHANAN and Coco sat upon the peak of one of the thousands of Black Range jagged points and looked down. The thin air of nightfall was cold. Coco shivered.

"They got fires. Why can't we have one?"

"They've got fires because they've got guns."

"And people. Lots of people."

"And Dolly Stone." He arose and jogged in place for a moment. "Wish I had my old field glasses. We got to get closer."

"Closer we get, the more trouble we're in."

"Uh-huh. Come on," said Buchanan.

They went down the slope. Locating the Masters camp had been too easy. Now it was a question of strategy, and Buchanan did not underestimate his opponent. The fires they had made were an invitation to the dance, he thought. They felt safe enough atop their little mesa to fight off the insufficient numbers on the side of Longbo. And—they had Dolly Stone.

When he could discern the details of the encampment he recognized the pattern. They had tents such as were used by railway workers. Each had its own little fire; the men made their own coffee, kept a constant watch. There was a big blaze before the largest of the tents, centrally located. He looked closely, squinting.

There were two folding chairs. In one sat Masters. In the other sat Dolly. Nearby were four men, each with a rifle at hand.

Masters knew his business. There would be no concerted attack upon the mesa so long as Dolly was exposed to it. If he were picked off by a rifle shot, his men would kill Dolly, break camp, and vanish.

That was his thinking. It would not work, Buchanan knew, if someone went berserk and did kill Masters. The men who killed Dolly would never get out of the mountains alive. But so long as they did not realize this and so long as Dolly must be saved, what did it matter?

He said to Coco, "There's only one way."

"And it ain't goin' to be good."

"Maybe not." Buchanan removed his gun

belt. He handed it to Coco. "Think of it as my friend. Protect it."

"I ain't goin' to shoot it."

"Didn't ask you to. You can stay right here and watch."

"You goin' in there?"

"No other way."

"They'll kill you, Tom. Or keep you tied up or somethin'."

"No," Buchanan said. He tapped the belt buckle wherein was hidden the deadly derringer. "They won't tie me up."

"You'd die in there just for that woman and her husband?"

Buchanan said, "Now, Coco, you know I never figure to get myself killed."

"There ain't no doubt about this one."

"Masters has got to know Vicenzio is somewhere about with Longbo and whoever else we could gather. He might even figure we sent down for Catlow."

"Why didn't we?"

"Catlow couldn't make it in time. But Vicenzio did send a messenger. Forget Catlow. This one is our wagon."

"And you goin' to pull it all alone?"

"Nope," said Buchanan. "I'm goin' to palaver."

He left without further discourse. He knew that despite his protests Coco would be close behind, yet far enough away so that he would not be seen nor heard. It was a problem of another kind. If they did attempt to kill him or hold him, Coco would be there with his bare fists, which could easily be the end of the world's greatest black prizefighter. Still he had to go on.

He went the most direct route, not concerned with concealment. When he came to the edge of the mesa a man peered down, pointing a rifle.

Buchanan called, "Tell Masters I'm here."

"Who's here?"

"Who did he expect, President Arthur?"

"You Buchanan?"

"I'm Buchanan."

The man called, "Mr. Masters, Buchanan's here."

Masters said, "Of course. Bring him to me."

It was a steep climb up the side of the mesa, but Buchanan noticed to his left there was an erosion which had bitten deep in some long ago age. Ignoring it for the present he clambered over the edge to where the man with the gun covered him. Two more came and took up positions, their fingers on the triggers.

Buchanan towered among them, arms half-raised. "I ain't loco. I'm here to talk."

Dolly called, "Oh, Buchanan! I knew you'd make it."

Masters lolled in his chair. "We all knew he'd

make it. Now that you're here, Buchanan, what's on your alleged mind?"

"Just wanted to hear from you what you got in your mind."

"You don't know? You're dumber than I thought."

"Guessin' ain't knowin'," Buchanan said. "You kidnapped Mrs. Stone, here." He approached them, the riflemen following at a prudent distance. In the background the man named Boston listened attentively, without comment. "There's a law against that."

"I'll deal with the law when the time comes," Masters said, waving a hand. "Meantime, all I want is peace and quiet for a few days."

"Uh-huh," said Buchanan. "Until the banks close in on Stone and the mine."

"Precisely."

"Your banks."

"Now, Buchanan, I don't own banks. Nobody owns all the banks. Surely you know that."

"What you own will do till somebody does. But look at it this way: You let Dolly go and we'll have a hard time pinnin' the theft of the engine on you—even if we could find it."

"Let the lady go? You are loco, at that, Buchanan."

"Am I? Sheriff Catlow don't think so. The people of Silver City will spread the word around—and they don't like you much. Kidnappin' a man's wife, that ain't the way it's done in this country."

For a moment Masters hesitated. He knew the code well enough. Women were sacred under frontier law. Then he laughed. "Mrs. Stone is unharmed. Isn't that true, Dolly?"

"He hasn't—uh—touched me," she said.

"You see. Now, I will make you a deal, Buchanan. Let Adah come in, of her own free will, and I'll turn Dolly over to you."

There was a moment of silence. Even the men employed by Masters looked stunned. Dolly turned white around the mouth.

"So that's it," Buchanan mused. "What a nice gentleman you are, Colin."

Dolly suddenly cried, "No! Don't do it! Let them do anything they want, but don't do it!"

"You see? She's a much nicer lady than you are a man," Buchanan said.

In the background Boston spat on the ground and walked away. There was a murmur among the workmen who were part of the expedition. Masters sensed his error at once. He waved the cheroot.

"A joke, of course. One hostage is as good as another. And you'll make the second, Buchanan."

"Uh-huh, I figured on that," said Buchanan. "So you don't want to talk about the law?"

"I have handled the law before. There are a

dozen ways. But you wouldn't know about that."

"Oh, I dunno," said Buchanan. "Been around a heap of law and lawmen in my time. They have different ideas from people like you."

"Money, you may have heard, makes the mare go." Masters contemptuously flicked his cigar.

A slip of wind came up. The hot ash landed on Dolly's dress. She cried out in pain.

Men started forward. Buchanan's hands went to his belt. From the near distance he heard the call of a wild bird which was not a bird.

He opened the clasp of his belt buckle. He took out the little gun. He took two steps, kicked the cigar from the hand of Masters, and lifted the little man by his coat collar. He pressed the derringer to his ear.

He said calmly, "Run, Dolly. Straight down the hill."

She picked up her skirts and ran. She stumbled, fell, then rolled over the edge of the mesa. They could hear her plunging through the brush.

Buchanan said, "You think I don't have guns down there? If so, then we know who's loco."

Masters choked inside his tight collar. "Don't shoot! Don't anybody shoot!"

Buchanan said, "Now, that's the only sensible thing you've said since I paid you this here little visit."

The men with the rifles backed off. If he tried

to take Masters along there was a chance that one of the true gunners could pick him off, Buchanan knew. If so, his reflex action might or might not kill Masters. In any case, he would be dead—and the engine undiscovered and Longbo in trouble, with or without his beloved wife.

He said, "I'm going to leave you with this, Colin, my boy. I'm going to leave you sit here and wonder. And after a while my folks will come and do what must be done. You ain't got enough men nor enough guns to stop us. And remember—you'll be the first to go when the time comes."

He walked to the edge of the mesa, still holding Masters in one hand. He turned as the riflemen followed him, paused a moment to grin at them, and tossed Masters as though he were a sack of meal, straight into the faces of the closest of them. Then he fired a shot to keep them off balance and dove into the crease he had noted earlier.

The moment he hit the crevice shots sounded, bullets splattered about him. He ran and leaped and was into the heavy undergrowth. He moved through it, knowing the terrain, guessing where Vicenzio was located by the sound he had heard earlier, the bird call.

Then he knew, because rifle fire was coming from that part of the mountain. The shots were aimed upward at the men on the edge of the mesa. Buchanan ran and in a few minutes' time all shooting had stopped. The Masters people had retreated from view. Vicenzio and Longbo saved their ammunition, not having high gun.

Buchanan found them in a rocky semishelter. Longbo demanded, "What happened to my Dolly? Why didn't you bring her with you?"

"You saw her get loose," said Buchanan. "Why didn't you go and get her?"

"He wouldn't let me," wailed Longbo, pointing a shaking finger at Vicenzio. "He says to wait and cover you."

"Vicenzio knows what this is all about," Buchanan told him. "And I wouldn't be surprised if here don't come Dolly now."

Coco was half-carrying her. There was little light from the moon as clouds whirled around the tops of the mountain range, but Buchanan had spotted them. She was weeping and wailing and generally acting the fool. Coco deposited her, shaking his head. Longbo ran to put his arm around her.

Coco said, "That lady's a handful. First off, she was so scared she thought I was one of them."

"Did you have to hit her?" Buchanan asked hopefully.

"Naw, just put my hand over her mouth."

Buchanan looked at Adah. "She did a brave thing up there. Masters offered to swap . . .

Dolly for you. She wouldn't hear of it."

"I told you before," Adah said softly. "There's a lot of good in her."

Vicenzio came closer. "Masters offered to exchange Mrs. Stone for Adah?"

"This is an old story," Adah said flatly. "There was a time when Masters supported my mother. Actually, he paid for my schooling."

"I do not understand this," said Vicenzio.

Buchanan said hastily, "Another time, my boy, another time. Right now, let me ask you, are we any better off than we were before?"

"Why, yes. We can attack."

"Attack a mesa full of armed men with this bunch?" Buchanan shook his head. "I looked them over. They got enough gunners to pick us off if we rush 'em. All he has to do is sit up there and wait."

Adah said, "The bank loans."

"That's it. Time is all it takes. He's got all the tickets right now."

"If we found the engine?"

"Who'd put it together and make it work?" Buchanan asked.

There was gloomy silence.

"How can all this be done in the time we have?" asked Adah.

Vicenzio gave forth with another of his bird calls. A stripling Apache came shyly from the brush. He wore only leggins, a breech clout, moccasins, and the traditional red headband.

"My nephew," Vicenzio said. "We go to my people with this problem."

"Can't ask that," Buchanan replied.

Vicenzio said, "They come from the north. With fire arrows. Dynamite sticks from the mine."

"It's not their fight," Adah protested.

"It is Buchanan's fight. And he is correct: rather Longbo Stone than this Masters."

He spoke to the youth, who nodded gravely and turned and ran in the direction of the mine.

"Fire arrows," said Buchanan. "Uh-huh. Things from the past. There's been a long dry spell. These tents up there must be dry."

"A distraction," Vicenzio said. "Then we go up."

"There's that little old gully. Know the one I mean?"

"I know it well."

"That just might do it. One thing, I don't want their mechanics killed if we can help it. Goin' to have to save 'em to put the engine back in runnin' order."

Coco said, "Leave it to me, I seen one of 'em; he didn't like what Masters was sayin'. He walked away. Heavyset fella. I'll choose him."

"You were that close when I was palaverin'?" demanded Buchanan. "You mighta got killed."

"Yeah. So might you," Coco retorted. He

clumsily unbuckled Buchanan's gun belt. "Here. Scared me jest to wear it."

Buchanan said, "Scares me to be without it at a time like this. Now all we got to do is wait. And like always, that's the hardest part."

They rested as best they could. Longbo and Dolly seemed to be having a serious talk apart from the others. Adah sat close to Vicenzio, smiling up at him. Buchanan stretched out alongside his friend Coco and tilted his hat over his eyes. If he could keep his mind from working he might get twenty winks, he thought.

He could not do so.

Colin Masters was struggling to regain stature among his men. The gunman named Corbin stood at his side.

"We're safe here," declared Masters. "Every man have his gun ready for an attack. Let them fire first. I'll show them the law is on our side."

"Yeah. Only you-all stole the engine," said Corbin.

"Nobody can prove it. When the time comes to put it to work, I'll have lawyers on hand."

Boston again spat expressively. "You got lawyers, all right. But they aren't here."

"The hell with all law," said Corbin. "Lost good men out there. The rest of my boys will remember that. They'll get even. Let those people try to come up here and we'll take the risks."

He stalked away. He had a dozen men under his command. Masters looked at Boston.

"Where's your gun?"

"Colin, I've worked for you a long time. I've done a lot of things off color, yeah, crooked. But you never knew me to kill anyone."

"You've killed a hundred Chinks on the railroads."

"They died. I didn't kill 'em. I don't shoot people."

"You may have to this time."

Boston said, "To defend my life, maybe yes. That Buchanan, he showed you something, Colin. I never saw you like this."

"Like what?"

"Uncertain. Nervous. Maybe scared."

"You're a damn fool, Boston. Nothing scares me. I've been through a hundred tough spots without being scared."

"Sure, I've been there. This time, your ball team was beaten. You've lost face in Silver City, Santa Rita, Encinal. That could go all the way to Santa Fe."

"Bosh! My influence goes all the way to Washington and you know it. I've done more for the West than ten Buchanans. What I want, I get!"

Boston said, "Up until now. It's a grand journey you've made. I made part of it with you. But what have we got?"

"Everything. What can a man want?"

Boston said, "Peace of mind. A home."

"I've got four homes. I keep my mind active. I know what I'm doing and where I'm going."

Boston shook his head. "Not me."

"You can quit whenever you want, you know," said Masters angrily.

"When I sign on, I keep my word," Boston told him. "I just have a feeling that I'd like to know the end, what it all means."

"It means a better world. It means getting what you want. It means . . ." Masters broke off. The girl was in his mind, Adah. He could not get the vision of her at the baseball game from his memory. He had partially seen her grow up; he knew she was different from other females. He wanted to explore that difference. He wanted her to submit, to go to her knees. And he realized that she did not like him, had never liked him, that now she might, indeed, hate him. He could not bear the thought. He ended, "It means that we have a goal and we work toward it."

"I'd like to know the goal," said Boston. He turned away. "I'll talk to my men. They don't like the idea of dying in this godforsaken mountain country. Oh, they'll fight if they have to. But you can't make them like it."

Masters walked around the encampment. The fires were all banked. The sentries were all posted. Corbin's men were strategically placed.

All that was needed was to hold the fort.

Yet the words of Boston lingered in his mind. He had known the man for ten years as a trusted employee. He had used him in many ways, and Boston had always responded. Now, in the chill of this high country he sensed a change.

The ball game had been a galling experience. He could only counter with a victory over Longbo, the acquisition of the mine, the defeat of Buchanan.

He remembered the feeling of utter helplessness when Buchanan had seized him. He had not been afraid to lose his life. He had suffered keen humiliation. He had sensed the dregs of defeat. Temporary, to be sure, but he could not endure the thought of losing. He lit a cheroot and walked around the perimeter of the mesa, hands behind his back, smoking furiously. Boston had been right, he admitted: He was off balance for the moment. He would hold on here until that feeling went away, he told himself with fierce determination.

The Apache boy suddenly appeared. He spoke in Vicenzio's ear. Buchanan set his hat firmly on his head and hitched up his cartridge belt. The time had come, and he always felt exhilaration when action was in prospect. It was a strange thing. He desired peace. All his life he had been forced to fight to attain it. The enjoyment of it was perverse. It was part of his life, of the fact of the West, where law and order could not quite reach.

Vicenzio asked, "You think the gully?"

"For a start. The women should go to the mine." He went to Longbo. Adah and her mother stood with the thin man. "It's time. You women should go with the boy, to the mine."

Adah shook her head. She moved close to Vicenzio. "You can't fight our battle without me."

Dolly, bedraggled in her long rumpled dress, her hair disarranged, picked up one of the rifles Vicenzio had retrieved. "I've shot one of these before, Buchanan. We're all past foolin' people now. You know what I been through in this world. Bo, here, he's good. I'll stick along."

It would put extra pressure on the men, Buchanan knew. Yet there was no way to prevent it.

Vicenzio said, "The boy would like to remain with us. He is not yet a full warrior. It is his chance."

Buchanan sighed. "Men, women, and children. A hell of a way to do battle."

Longbo said, "Me and Dolly talked it over. After what she heard and saw up there she figures it's all over any old way. Masters has got us. So we take what we can from him and his'n."

Buchanan looked at the two ballplayers from the East. "I don't have to ask. You came this far. I know you're not going to leave the party."

Mallet said, "In the barber shops I used to read about the wild West. Now I'm in it. What's there for us anywhere in the world? A good fight is enough."

Buchanan nodded. Coco stood with his hands behind his back. There was no reason to question him. It depended greatly upon the Apaches, how they responded. He said, "Okay, let's try and make it to the gully. The fireworks should start any minute now."

He led them, single file, keeping low in the darkness. The clouds were scudding above, and he hoped for the moon. He did not like a night fight; too much was left to chance.

He came to the crevice. There would be someone up above with a gun. He hesitated. Alone he would be able to eliminate one man—but what then? The forces on the mesa were simply too strong.

He checked his motley command. Never had he led such a strange crew. He looked again at the sky. A sudden moon would reveal their position, but he thought they could lie low enough and still enough until the action began.

It came as suddenly as a flash flood. The air became full of fire. He had almost forgotten the strange, eerie, wild sound of the Apaches at war. Their screams shook the very earth as the arrows rained down on the encampment above.

Buchanan went up the slope of the gully at top speed. Because the attack came from the north, he counted upon all faces being turned in that direction. The gunman he had expected was plain to be seen, mouth agape, staring. Buchanan reached out and put his big hand over the man's mouth, struck him with the barrel of his Colt and slung him backward to the tender mercies of those behind him. Then he crouched, gun in hand, surveying the scene.

Fires had sprung up all over the mesa. Men were running in all directions, including into one another. He could hear the shrill voice of Masters but could not distinguish the words. At any rate, he thought, a single command would not bind a band of mercenaries plus ordinary workmen together.

He beckoned and Coco came up. "If we can find Masters, grab him and take him down."

"Couldn't find nobody in this mess," complained Coco.

There was a loud explosion. On the other edge of the mesa, men fell, shouted. The flames leaped higher. The moon came from behind a bank of clouds, and there was light enough for Buchanan to pick a target. One of Corbin's men saw him and lifted his gun. Buchanan shot him through the chest.

Now Vicenzio was over the rim, remaining low, pumping the rifle. Men fell. Corbin was gathering his force together, Buchanan saw. There lay the danger, a concerted defense.

Still the Apaches yowled and sent their arrows. Corbin had his men grouped and was looking for a target. Mallet and Keen and Longbo crept over the rim. The women came behind, Longbo pushing them prone, exhorting them to make scant targets. Still, Buchanan saw, they were firing at anything that moved.

It was Corbin who first saw Buchanan. He shouted an order and knelt, aiming his rifle.

Coco, obeying orders, was searching for Masters. He came past Corbin, reached out one fist and knocked the gunman ten feet across the mesa. Buchanan fired and one of the cohorts of the gunner fell. Vicenzio, seeing the situation clearly, fired three times. Corbin, rising groggily, yelled, "You and me, Buchanan. I got no rifle."

Buchanan said, "It's a deal."

The gunman went for his revolver. Buchanan drew the Colt and snapped off two shots. Corbin staggered, threw out his arms, and fell on his back.

Now the fires were everywhere. Men ran for their lives. Buchanan used his biggest, most powerful voice.

"This way! Drop your guns and you'll live! Keep 'em and you may as well burn!"

A few of them staggered toward him, dropping guns as they came. He sent them to the gully. Longbo and the women covered them. The man named Boston came walking, hands raised, Coco close behind.

"You win, Buchanan," he said. "I'm no fighter."

"Go down and stay with Longbo," Buchanan ordered. "Where is Masters?"

Boston shrugged. "He's no coward. Prob'ly looking for a chance to get you before he goes."

Buchanan said, "Can you get some of your workers to go with you?"

"They have no stomach for this."

"Then take them down."

He went in among the burning tents. He saw Masters, then lost him in a swirling mass of smoke. He choked a bit as the wind shifted. There were still some fighters left. One fired at him. Buchanan cut his legs from under him with one shot, then as the man tried to lift his revolver reluctantly shot him in the head.

At that moment a bullet tugged at his shoulder. He spun and knelt, peering. He saw Masters again.

The millionaire was blackened with smoke, scorched by fire. He had a rifle and was aiming it at Buchanan, trying to get in another shot.

Buchanan called, "Better drop it. This ain't your kind of business."

"You did it, damn you. You and your damn Indians."

"And a couple of black men and two women," Buchanan said. His arm was beginning to sting. "Put down the gun, Colin. Your hand's played out."

Masters tried to aim through the smoke. "I'll see you in hell, Buchanan!"

There was nothing to do but shoot. Buchanan took careful aim, waited a moment, then triggered the Colt.

The gun flew from the hands of Masters. At almost the same instant Coco reappeared. Huge, strong hands lifted the little man.

"I got him," Coco said. "Now what do I do with him?"

"Take him down below. I've got use for him."

"You goin' to let him live?"

"I'm goin' to send him to jail," said Buchanan. "Just a lesson for others like him."

Coco said, "Now, that's real nice of you, Tom." He carried Masters as though he were a loaf of bread. He moved quickly toward the gully down which were filing men under the direction of Boston.

Buchanan moved his arm. The bullet hadn't struck bone, he thought. He mopped blood with his kerchief and walked around the mesa, reloading the Colt.

The fires were dying. He called out in Spanish to the Apaches below.

"The work is done. Return to the mine. You will be rewarded and your children will be rewarded for your work this night."

There was one wild yell, mocking, disbelieving. Then there was silence to the north. It only remained to dig up Engine 69 and regroup at the Longbo Mine. The wound didn't hurt much. It was one of the many and he had been lucky. An experienced shot would have killed him, given the chance that Masters had. He walked down to have words with Boston and Colin Masters. He already had guessed the hiding place of Engine 69. It only remained to get it together on time—which was problem enough. Time was short; Buchanan was sleepy and hungry and wounded. Still he felt good. The battle was over and there had been only one slight casualty— himself.

9.

MEN worked at the mine. It was early morning and Buchanan had not slept and he had eaten only cold food. His arm ached. Adah had bandaged it with tender care, but it still hurt. Time was passing and he wanted Engine 69 put back together. They had dug it up, brought it in, and Boston's mechanics were working under the guns of Mallet, Keen, and Longbo. Colin Masters was locked up in the workmen's quarters, under the watchful eyes of the Mexicans whose jobs he had threatened. The remaining gunmen were disarmed and resigned.

Mary came with a steaming bowl of soup. Buchanan accepted it gratefully and drank deep.

The girl said, "Sure and the Missus is changed

entirely. She asked me to bring this to you. Asked me, mind you."

"When big trouble comes, some people find themselves," Buchanan said.

"Things will be different around here, then?"

"Better," he promised her.

He went to Boston. "I want the men to work faster. Do you understand?"

"You've got the guns," said the foreman. He went to where the men were laying track and re-assembling Engine 69.

Adah and Vicenzio were, as usual, together, sitting on the steps of the house. Buchanan drifted close, shamelessly eavesdropping.

"I am afraid," Vicenzio was saying.

"I'm not," she replied with spirit.

"My people need me. I am Apache."

She said, "And I have Indian blood. I felt it when I came to these hills."

"But you cannot live with my people. They would not understand. They would not accept it."

"We will see about that. I am willing to try."

He said with difficulty, "Adah . . . I love you."

"And I love you." She took his hand. "It is enough for a start. We can be married at the mission."

Buchanan slipped away. As she had said, it was a start. The Apaches had gone back to the old place, but Nogalla was leaning against a tall tree alone, surveying the scene. Buchanan went to him.

"Your son wishes to marry the girl."

"Yes."

"It is not good for them to live in the old place."

"No."

"Vicenzio could return to school. There will be plenty of money."

"Yes."

"Then he could come to the mountains. There is much to be learned. Longbo will be a rich man. He has said that his land is your land. Do you believe him?"

"Do you?"

"I believe my friend."

Nogalla said, "You came here to help him. You helped us. We were able to help you. It is good."

"It is good," said Buchanan.

"We are not completely ignorant," said Nogalla. "We have seen the cars. The Apaches could never bring down the silver to the mills; this is not our way. It will be done, but we can have no part of it."

"Longbo will see to all that."

"I think I believe."

"Then you'll talk to Vicenzio?"

"I will talk to him."

Longbo was handing his gun to a laborer,

starting for the house. Buchanan followed, noting that Boston had the men working at the double.

Dolly had donned another costume, her hair was in place, she sat in the parlor. When Longbo entered she ran to him and kissed him.

"Thank God we're all in one piece." She saw Buchanan and paused. Then she said, "Your arm. You should see a doctor."

"In time," Buchanan told her. "Everything in good time. I got a long rest comin' to me anyhow." He addressed Longbo. "I made a heap of promises to Nogalla in your name."

"Depend on me," said Longbo. "They saved our bacon."

"Then there's Adah. And Vicenzio."

"I know," interposed Dolly. "Funny how a body can change opinion, ain't it now?"

"She's more like back in Frisco," beamed Longbo. "She sees things like from another place. I mean—"

"He means I've quit playin' the lady," said Dolly bluntly. "It was a fine game, I thought. It was somethin' I always wanted to be . . . a lady with jewelry and money and all that. Even on this mountain, I wanted it. Then when things started to go bad I near went crazy."

"Then you came along," Longbo said to Buchanan. "I ain't never goin' to forget that, nohow, no time, not ever."

Buchanan said, "What are friends for?"

"Not to get shot up," said Dolly. "Not to show us how the Apaches could be friendly."

"Not to put up cash when everything's goin' out the window and the friend's been all kinds of a damn fool," said Longbo.

"It worked out," said Buchanan uncomfortably. "I'll make a profit if the mine pans out. Nothin' to it." He found he was carrying the empty bowl. He made a gesture and took it into the kitchen.

Mary said, "Here's some meat and potatoes, real hot it is."

He ate. His arm was hurting more and more, and he was afraid it was infected. He had some Indian herbs in his saddlebags, which were in the quarters, he remembered.

He finished the food and checked the work on the engine. Boston knew his business; the parts were being reassembled with care and speed. He went on past the armed guards and into the building.

Masters was sitting on a cot, reading an old copy of *Police Gazette*. He had regained his former arrogance, Buchanan sensed at once.

"So you won your little battle," he said. "How does it feel to have beaten Colin Masters?"

Buchanan rummaged in the saddlebag, found what he was looking for. He took off his shirt and tenderly removed the bandage Adah had applied. He began dabbing ointment from a vial, causing the wound to smart a little.

"Hell, we beat your ball team, we beat your gunners, and we're goin' to beat the banks. That has to feel pretty doggone good, wouldn't you think?"

"Look at you," said Masters. "Scars all over your body from fighting the battles of other people. You're a damned fool after all, Buchanan."

"Could be." He rebandaged the wound as best he could, knowing Adah would complete the job. He asked, "I note you kept your ballplayers outa the fight. They in town?"

"They'll be all right."

"Uh-huh," Buchanan agreed. "I don't expect they'd mind takin' on a couple of black men, now, would they? Seein' as the blacks would make 'em stronger and better."

"Are you thinking of taking over the Westerners?" Masters laughed.

The door opened. Sheriff Catlow entered.

"Been expectin' you," said Buchanan. "Here's your prisoner."

"Ha!" Masters sneered. "Take me in. See how long you keep me."

"A few years, maybe," Catlow said. "Got a nice bill of particulars agin you, Masters. Kidnappin' a lady. Stealin' property. Hirin' gunmen to fight citizens. Furthermore, there's a man sent me a telegram from Santa Fe sayin' there's some funny business with a bank or two. Seems one of your people got scared and squawked to the Governor."

"You can't scare me!"

Catlow said, "Scare you? I imagine the lawyers will be all over the place defendin' you. Frisco lawyers. They don't count for much in New Mexico, though."

"We'll see about that. Governor Wallace—"

"It was Wallace said to hold you," observed Catlow mildly. He took a pair of handcuffs from his belt. "Brought up a carriage to take you down in style."

"You can't do this to me!" He jumped to his feet. "Nobody can do this to Colin Masters."

Catlow snapped on the cuffs. "It's just been done. And for my money, it couldn't happen to a worse fella. Come on, Masters, take a drive with me."

Buchanan followed them outside, struggling into his shirt. The men stopped work to stare. Boston barked an order to them, and they resumed their task. Buchanan watched the carriage start down the tracks.

Boston asked, "Am I next?"

"Could be," said Buchanan. "But if you get the engine runnin' and the ore goes down on time—well, I know a trail to Mexico. They can always use men like you down there. Might even give you the name of a friend."

Boston grabbed a spanner from a workman.

"Get out of my way and let me show you how this is done!" he said.

Buchanan went searching for Adah. He found her alone, a bit pale but composed. She bandaged his arm again.

"Nogalla is talking to Vicenzio," she said.

"This I want to hear. And maybe add a few words."

The two Apaches were among the trees, facing one another. Nogalla was speaking.

"You were a good leader. I wanted you to see how we lived. You had the school, you had the mountains. You learned both ways. Which will prevail?"

"My place is with the people."

"My son, you are not the chief. I am the chief. You will take this woman. You will return to the school. You will learn. Then you may come back, and the people may profit by your learning, the young people. By then we old ones will have gone on. Then you will be needed. Now—you are not needed."

Vicenzio stood on one foot, then the other, like any schoolboy being spoken to by his father.

Buchanan said, "Also, you'll be playin' ball. The Westerners, they won't have a boss. Silver City will be more'n proud to take them over. I see a league bein' formed. I see where bein' a good ballplayer will bring much honor to all.

And 'specially to an Apache, a future leader of his people."

"A child's game." But Vicenzio was weakening. "A married man playing games. And going to school."

"Because your father and Longbo and me, we say that is the way it's goin' to be," Buchanan told him, not mincing his words.

"It is so!" thundered Nogalla. "Farewell, my son. You will not come to the old place until you are ready."

He turned and walked away, up into the mountains. Vicenzio took one step to follow, then stopped. He stared at Buchanan.

"Is this right?"

"Friend, I don't claim to know right from wrong a whole heap of the time. But now—I'm tellin' you. It ain't just right, it's the only way you got to go."

After a moment a hint of a smile adorned the handsome dark features of the young man. "I am being forced to marry, to attend school, to play a game. Buchanan, you are a man of many qualities. This I have always known."

"And that's some papa you got there," Buchanan reminded him. "Now run along and tell your troubles to the gal."

He watched Vicenzio run to join Adah.

Coco and the two ballplayers were guarding the workmen. Buchanan joined them.

He said, "Well, we got the boy straightened out. Now about baseball."

"No way for us to go," said Mallet. "Maybe we could get a job in the mine."

Buchanan said, "I'm about to take over the Westerners. They become the Silver City Stars. A black manager—now that would be a novelty! Mallet, you got the big mouth; Keen will be your assistant."

"How you goin' to do that?"

"Easy. Masters will be in jail. Some of those dudes will run . . . like Scar Donlin. But enough'll stay on, show 'em how it's goin' to be. You mind that little fella, Billy Button?"

"He shot the gunman."

"He thinks he's a big sport," Buchanan told them. "He's got plenty of money and plenty of time. Among us, you-all will get well paid. But you better have the best team in the West."

Mallet gave Buchanan a skeptical look. "Me? A manager?"

"Well, maybe Catlow'll have to use the title. But he's a smart man. He'll know how to handle it."

Keen said, "You know what? This here is so much better than where we have been that it's like heaven on earth."

"Let's try and keep it that way." Buchanan sighed. "I'm a peaceable man. Nothin' I'm goin' to like better than to rest awhile, hunt, fish—and watch ball games."

Boston was accomplishing his task. Buchanan found a piece of paper and scribbled a name on it and handed it to him. "Down Chihuahua way," he said. "Tell them Buchanan sent you."

Boston wiped away sweat. "You think they can put Masters in jail? Really?"

"Man gets too big, he overreaches himself," said Buchanan. "I'll be sendin' a telegram to Governor Wallace myself. Friend of mine. Always writin', that man, but he's got a lot of honest horse sense."

"Colin Masters in jail?" Boston shook his head. "Impossible for me to picture that."

"Time'll tell. One thing—he won't ever be the big man in this Territory, you can lay to that." He went back to the house. Adah and Vicenzio were in the parlor, and one glance told him all was well between them.

He went to the kitchen. Mary dimpled at him. He said, "Things seem under control here, don't they?"

"Ah, and thanks to you, Mr. Buchanan."

"If you ever need a friend, let it be known. You're a good girl, Mary."

She threw her arms around him and kissed him soundly. "And if you ever want me for anything at all, at all, just let that be known," she whispered in his ear.

He patted her absently. Maybe he had not recently had an offer as good, but his mind was on other matters. He ambled out the back door. The arm felt better already, thanks to the magic salve of the Indian girl from up north whom he had once befriended.

He went to the lean-to stable, and Nightshade, long neglected, whinnied up a storm. He said, "Quiet now. Everything's workin' out fine."

He managed to saddle up. He rode out and stopped beside Coco.

"You goin' without me?" demanded the prize-fighter.

"It's time," Buchanan said. "When your friends get settled in Silver, you come on to Encinal. I'll be there."

"You goin' to see that baby before I do." Coco purely adored the Buttons youngster.

"He'll be waitin' for you," said Buchanan. "I aim to sleep in a hotel bed tonight. I aim to eat the Widow's place out of business."

As he rode off, Coco called, "That Widder's got her eye on you, so watch yourself."

Well, the Widow wasn't so bad after all, thought Buchanan. He waved good-bye and rode down the trail.

He still didn't quite care for the look of the shiny rails. They were changing his country. He knew it had to happen; he had just helped it to happen. But he didn't like it.

WESTERNS

☐	AMBUSH AT JUNCTION ROCK—MacLeod	P3471	1.25
☐	THE APACHE HUNTER—Shirreffs	P3479	1.25
☐	BARREN LAND SHOWDOWN—Short	13659-0	1.25
☐	BOWMAN'S KID—Shirreffs	13599-3	1.25
☐	CHARROI—Whittington	13703-1	1.25
☐	CIMARRON JORDAN—Braun	P3201	1.25
☐	DAKOTA BOOMTOWN—Castle	P3521	1.25
☐	DAY OF THE BUZZARD—Olsen	P3530	1.25
☐	THE EASY GUN—Parsons	13712-0	1.25
☐	GRINGO—Foreman	13555-1	1.25
☐	THE GUNSHARP—Cox	13549-7	1.25
☐	HE RODE ALONE—Frazee	13581-0	1.25
☐	THE KID FROM RINCON—Moore	13612-4	1.25
☐	KING FISHER'S ROAD—Rifkin	13711-2	1.25
☐	A MAN NAMED YUMA—Olsen	13616-7	1.25
☐	THE MANHUNTER—Shirreffs	13728-7	1.25
☐	THE MARAUDERS—Shirreffs	13723-6	1.50
☐	SMOKY VALLEY—Hamilton	13677-9	1.50
☐	TO HELL AND TEXAS—Lutz	13597-7	1.25
☐	TOP MAN WITH A GUN—Patten	13705-8	1.25
☐	WHITE APACHE—Forrest	13754-6	1.25

Buy them at your local bookstores or use this handy coupon for ordering:

Louis L'Amour

THE NUMBER ONE SELLING WESTERN AUTHOR OF ALL TIME. Mr. L'Amour's books have been made into over 25 films including the giant bestseller HONDO. Here is your chance to order any or all direct by mail.

☐ CROSSFIRE TRAIL	13836-4	1.50
☐ HELLER WITH A GUN	13831-3	1.25
☐ HONDO	13830-5	1.50
☐ KILKENNY	13821-6	1.50
☐ LAST STAND AT PAPAGO WELLS	13880-1	1.50
☐ SHOWDOWN AT YELLOW BUTTE	13893-3	1.50
☐ THE TALL STRANGER	13861-5	1.50
☐ TO TAME A LAND	13832-1	1.50
☐ UTAH BLAINE	P3382	1.25

Buy them at your local bookstores or use this handy coupon for ordering:

FAWCETT PUBLICATIONS, P.O. Box 1014, Greenwich Conn. 06830

Please send me the books I have checked above. Orders for less than 5 books must include 60c for the first book and 25c for each additional book to cover mailing and handling. Orders of 5 or more books postage is Free. I enclose $_____ in check or money order.

Mr/Mrs/Miss _____

Address _____

City _____ State/Zip _____

Please allow 4 to 5 weeks for delivery. This offer expires 6/78.   A-1